The Blue Parrot

The Blue Parrot

John Moore

Ekstasis  Editions

Canadian Cataloguing in Publication Data

Moore, John
   The blue parrot

      Novel
      ISBN 1-896860-52-4

      I. Title.
      PS8576.O6142B6   1999   C813'.54   C99-910350-4
      PR9199.3.M66B6   1999

Cover Art: A detail from a painting by Michael Lewis
Author Portrait: *Portrait of John Moore* by Grenville Newton

Published in 1999 by:
Ekstasis Editions Canada Ltd.   Ekstasis Editions
Box 8474, Main Postal Outlet   Box 571
Victoria, B.C. V8W 3S1   Banff, Alberta ToL oCo

THE CANADA COUNCIL | LE CONSEIL DES ARTS
FOR THE ARTS | DU CANADA
SINCE 1957 | DEPUIS 1957

The Blue Parrot has been published with the assistance of a grant from the Canada Council and the Cultural Services Branch of British Columbia.

For Mary,
for everything.

Chapter 1

It was dark in the Blue Parrot Lounge, but not dark enough to give me an excuse for staring hard when Lisa came in that first time. I was doing a little of anything — polishing glasses, giving the steel sinks a wipe, cutting fruit I'd only have to throw out at closing time — things bartenders do when they have nothing to do but keep all the blood in their bodies from settling below their knees. I was doing it all without running into myself in the coffin-size space behind the bar.

It was getting slowly but steadily darker in the Blue Parrot. Since the hotel it served had been built in the days when guardians of public morality in British Columbia decreed the sight of people consuming alcoholic beverages to be a danger to the common weal, there were no windows at all in the beer parlour. As a concession to the ostensibly more civilized environment of the Blue Parrot cocktail lounge, its outer wall was pierced by a single round porthole, about twenty-four inches in diameter, set high enough into the brick facade that it might offer a glimpse of the interior only to those impressionable passersby equipped with stilts. Suspended within that circle of grimy glass was the insignia of the establishment — the stylized outline of a parrot, like a crude tattoo, aglow in ancient pale blue neon.

Inside, it was cheaper to dim the lights than renovate. The old red brick hotel stood two steep blocks up from the North Vancouver waterfront and had been there almost as long as the place had a name.

The original architect must have had delusions of squalor, since it was impossible to imagine the building ever having been new. High arched windows, trimmed in gray brick and made up of vertical lozenges of glass whose darkened leading inevitably suggested bars, made it look like a Victorian madhouse-set from a B-movie.

Thanks to occasional contracts at the shipyards and a few slowly strangling light industrial shops, the beer parlour still did a reasonable trade, but the whole area was being steadily re-developed. Sawmills, cement plants and shacky workshops had been replaced by office and apartment buildings constructed of steel, pastel-painted concrete and glass, arranged in what architects conspicuously considered to be interesting shapes. Blue-plate diners gave way to skylit, fern-dappled bistros and delicatessens serving designer coffees, juices and mineral waters and diet suggestions of the day.

Vacant lots that punctuated the old waterfront used to be dumping grounds for large rusting parts of obscure machinery and discarded items of furniture. Eviscerated sofas and armchairs nestled among the nettles like a hobo's living room suite, occupied on summer evenings by punks too young and winos too poor to drink in sanctioned surroundings, with the odd glue-sniffer clutching a plastic bag to his face like an oxygen mask, rounding out the guest list. Now the waste lots were being paved for paid parking, every foot of useless ground filled in with bark mulch, stunted juniper and shrub cedars.

As the bright new aggressively geometrical buildings rose from the waterfront like a Cubist tidal wave, the old hotel deteriorated at the same rate as the property increased in value. The owners, an offshore real estate holding company, didn't have to spend a dime. The night Lisa came in, this economic paradox was the subject of the usual running seminar held by a few of the regulars in a corner booth.

"How can she be worth more, when the old girl's ready to fall into the street, like a pissed slag on Welfare Wednesday? Answer me that..."

The speaker, who claimed a comprehensive knowledge of the sliding scale of depreciation as applied to old cars, old boats and old whores, was shouted down.

"It's what you call your Law of Supply and Demand..."

"It's what you call your Free Enterprise..."

"It's what you call your Capitalistic System..."

Confronted with an irrational truth, he shook his head and muttered, "No wonder the world's going to Hell with a first class ticket."

A funereal silence settled over the table while the occupants pondered the inevitable day to come when their alcoholic autopilot would guide them to their old watering-hole, like a herd of migrating wildebeest through a dust storm, only to find a huge boarded-up emptiness, identified by a posted Development Permit Application as the future home of some gleaming glass and steel monument to mortal change.

I could barely make them out in the gloom, but I knew their voices, knew from the tone and slur how many rounds they'd had and how many more they were good for and, from the tinkle of melting ice in their glasses, when to bring the next. Most of the regulars in the Blue Parrot were just killing time. At least, that's what they called it, to help them avoid thinking about who was really killing who.

The darkness in the lounge was as forgiving to the customers as it was to the decor. Between the low lights and Yours Truly pouring the drinks, male and female patrons of the bar had been known to revise their birth certificates by as much as a decade on a lucky night. If there was misrepresentation, it was usually mutual and not the kind of thing anyone wants to bring up first thing in the morning.

"My motto is," one of the ladies told me, "Keep the lights low and a robe handy."

Lisa didn't need any help from the dimmer switch. At a glance I guessed that, like me, she was about to step into the cool shade of forty, out of the glaring sunshine of youth. She looked like one of those girls who'd developed early and probably been a heart-breaker in high school, dating eighteen year old Industrial Arts dropouts who owned hot cars when she was only fifteen.

Girls like that, who go from twelve to twenty in what seems

like one golden summer, never know boys their own age exist. From them, boys such as I was learn their first and most painful lessons in the fine art of self-laceration we call love. Moping, sulking, pimply wrecks, barely able to stutter in Her presence, they stifle adolescent tears with pillows and chronic erections with practised hands. Love is always hell on the laundry.

What the boys don't know is that two great forces are silently plotting revenge for all that unrequited love. Time and gravity are cruel to those early-blooming girls, like the last frost that kills the crocus and daffodil seduced by Vancouver's frequent false springs. In supermarkets, years later, I've recognized a few former subjects of my adoration, girls who once made me believe it might actually be possible to die of love. With a kind of sad satisfaction I've noted their pasty faces, the bloated waists I'd've cut off my hand for the chance to put my arm around, cellulite-padded thighs I'd've sold my soul to lie between.

Listening to their harried mothers' voices muttering metric conversion tables and alternating snarled threats with helpless bribes to discourage their squealing brats from plundering the aisles, it's occurred to me that marriage is a form of revenge — the revenge men take for having fallen in love with loveliness itself and the revenge women take for being loved for that alone.

Some men might've said Lisa's best years were behind her. Her beauty had a broken-in look. I didn't mind it. Most things are better when they're broken-in — engines, blue jeans, guitars. The trouble with people is that the time between broken-in and worn out is too damn short.

Lisa could still make every glass in the room pause in mid-air and she wasn't even well-dressed. The brown leather jacket and jeans she wore were a long time off the rack, but I sensed stomachs being sucked in, ties straightened, thinning hair patted and palmed into place all over the room.

When her eyes adjusted to the darkness, she checked out the lounge with a half-expectant expression, pretending to be looking for someone she was supposed to meet. A lot of people who come into bars alone do that. Then she came to the bar and ordered a glass of white wine in a hesitant, almost-but-not-quite little girl voice.

"Are you sure that's what you want?"

The Blue Parrot isn't the kind of bar where you order an amusing Napa chardonnay and assorted antipasti. She gave me a puzzled half-smile.

"Is there something wrong with that?"

"Not if you're stripping the paint off a car," I said with a shrug.

"It's that bad?"

"Let me put it this way. It's been so long since anybody ordered a glass of white wine in this bar that it would probably be better on fish'n chips." I held up a glass, posing like a connoisseur, "It's an impudent little porch-rat, with hints of hemlock and hellebore. A whisper of belladonna on the finish. A Chateau Socrates, I believe."

She gave me a smile laced with genuine rue.

"It sounds like the right stuff."

I set her up with a glass and got out of range.

"It's not the worst I've had, but it's a runner-up," she admitted when I got back from taking another round to the think-tank in the corner.

It was a slow night and I was covering the floor as well as the bar. Marion, the cocktail waitress of record, was on a long break, closeted in the other corner booth, patting the hand of one of her likewise fiftyish bottled-blonde cronies and establishing once and for all what total prick bastards men are.

"Nice place," Lisa commented, as if I'd decorated it myself.

The decor in the Blue Parrot, what you could see of it, was Pseudo-Polynesian with African Tribal accents, complete with black velvet paintings of dusky girls with large round eyes and larger and rounder breasts. It suited the customers, most of whom would have done the downstairs rec room exactly like it if they'd been the kind of people who could afford a six bedroom, three and a half bath Del Mar style split level in the suburbs up the hill.

I looked around like I'd never seen the place before in my life. "Yeah. Sort of Heart of Darkness by Trader Vic's."

"I meant," she said conspiratorily, "It seems like the kind of place where a girl can have a glass of wine without getting hit on every minute."

"Oh, you can still get hit on," I assured her, "But most of the guys who come in here can't hit as hard or as often as they used to."

She liked that, but I wasn't about to be suckered into patronizing myself. That leaves a worse taste in your mouth than the Blue Parrot's house wine. "So what's a low-rent bitch like you doing in a class joint like this?" I inquired nonchalantly.

She coughed a little wine and for a second I thought she might being going to return the rest for a refund the hard way, straight into my face. At least she wasn't drinking something on the rocks. Instead she came up laughing.

"Is that your best shot?"

"That's my only shot," I told her, "I don't hit at all."

"Not at all?" Her disappointment was almost convincing.

I shook my head. "I've danced my last tango in the minefield of love. Nothing but scar tissue and plastic from the waist down."

"Sure. Yeah." she said in mock disbelief, giving me a speculative look I liked in spite of myself.

Another time, I might have been tempted to take my cappezios off the hook and try a pas de deux with her. She had trouble, I could tell, and a woman in trouble always attracts men, usually the way the straggler in the herd draws wolves. At least the hamstrung caribou, alone and surrounded by a howling pack, knows it's time to go down fighting and take as many of the mangy fuckers with you as you can. Most people never get that chance, or don't recognize it, so they just get slowly eaten alive, a bite at a time.

Hope is the human weakness. Even as the great jaws are closing around our lives, we can't stop hoping that if we just pretend we don't see them, if we make ourselves very small and quiet, don't ask for too much, don't rock the boat or kick against the pricks, somehow the shadow will pass over us and everything will be alright.

It never works, of course. The mills of the gods, as they say, grind exceedingly fine to produce deluxe bone meal.

Mind you, women with trouble sometimes get the other kind of men, the gimpy Galahads who can't resist the lure of the damsel dungeoned in the dark tower of the soul, the dimestore knights errant, brandishing their five-in-one screwdriver and socket-set psychology, who believe that life is something you can fix, like a loose timing-chain or a broken alarm clock.

I'd shattered my share of lances on innocuous-looking windmills that turned out to be big and bad tempered giants. My armour was as thin as cigarette foil and the Dodge Charger I once briefly owned was on blocks in somebody's backyard, demonstrating a process of oxidization known as rust.

I'd taken up the religious life. I drank religiously.

Chapter 2

I never expected to see Lisa again. Most of the regulars at the Blue Parrot were a lot closer to worn out than she was and, like I said, it really wasn't a white wine drinker's kind of bar. We still sold a lot of rye; rye and Seven, rye and ginger, rye and coke, rye and water, shots of rye. Rye is the traditional Canadian whisky, but over the last decade or so sales have nosedived in favour of scotch, especially single malts, as if a belt or two of one of them would magically make you as suave as a Grenadier Guard in a shirt ad. Of course, we also sold a lot of vodka.

Colourless, odourless and essentially tasteless, vodka is the secret base from which we bartenders plot our revenge on the drinking world. We mix it with Clamato juice, a concoction which resembles a blend of fish slime and blood, to commemorate the multiple slicing and dicing of a Roman dictator. We mix it with Southern Comfort, sloe gin and orange juice just so giggling "ladies' night" hen parties can bat their lights at the bored stud waiter as they order a round of Sloe Comfortable Screws. We mix it with pineapple juice, cream and synthetic coconut dust and pump six of them into young girls in night clubs who can later be seen, supported by their mortified and sexually frustrated escorts, paving the parking lot with the curdled contents of their flat little stomachs. There are worse jobs than bartending. One of them is being a dry-cleaner on Monday morning.

The Blue Parrot

I like vodka. A straight shot, splashed into short wide Old-Fashioned glass crowded with cubes and topped off with ice water. If you leave it for a minute or two, listening to the soft crackle of the ice like a distant river breaking up in spring, it tastes just like very cold water with a faint heaviness suggestive of the pure mineralized streams that feed remote glacial lakes high above the tree line where not even insects or birds can live.

This is the ultimate drinker's drink; stripped of taste, colour, bouquet, all the pretensions that disguise the real business at hand. Sometimes, when I'd had just enough, I felt I achieved the cool neutral transparency of the spirit itself. It was a matter of fine measurement and timing, but then, most things are.

One of the transient tenants who passed through the old hotel during my tenure was a rounder whose girlfriend was a junkie whore. Sometimes he would use her outfit to crank a few c.c.'s of vodka straight into the line and get instantly shit-faced. That was a matter of fine measurement and timing, too. A c-hair too much and you could be instantly dead. You could spin a bottle of vodka out pretty far that way when you were between pogey cheques and the Duchess was too wasted to drag her ass down to the strip, he argued while inviting me to join him in an intravenous cocktail, but it wasn't drinking. When I woke up I had to agree with him. I still don't know what it was, but it wasn't drinking.

Secretly, I suppose I was glad when Lisa came back to the Blue Parrot a few nights later. This time she came straight to the bar and smiled because I had a glass of white wine set up right in front of me, like I'd been expecting her. Everybody loves that, whether they're winos or millionaires. For most people, having a bartender remember your name and what you drink is as close to fame as you're ever going to get.

After that, she came in regularly. Not every night, but a couple of times a week. Often enough for Marion, among others, to take notice.

"Here comes trouble," Marion said, one night soon after Lisa started turning up. I looked up to see that zipper-melting smile bearing down on me through the smoky gloom.

"I thought you were an expert on men," I muttered as I finished building her order and put up a glass of white wine with my other hand.

"Being an expert on men makes you an expert on women, whether you like it or not," Marion snapped back, switching away on her spike heels to make herself desperately charming to three sports who'd just witnessed Lisa's entrance and were twitching like hypnotized chickens.

I guess it was natural for Marion to resent Lisa. Marion had been a knockout in her time and, by Blue Parrot standards, still was. The heels did things for her long whippy legs and rounded rear that could still cause twenty year-old jocks to walk into lampstandards as they gaped. Her superstructure was a wordlessly eloquent testimonial to the underwire bra. With her cinched waist and tall blonde beehive hair, she always reminded me of one of those dangerously bright, deceptively delicate elongated wasps.

Yet Lisa's presence couldn't help but remind the room that Marion's time would forever be a decade before her own. The mouldering buzzards in the Blue Parrot's booths preened their draggled feathers for Lisa as they'd always done for Marion, but with new vigour. They even curbed their language, not completely, but the way they might in front of a grown daughter or niece. When they moved aside to let her pass, I swear a couple of them would have bowed, if they'd known how to do it without knocking over a table full of drinks.

I liked Lisa, but I was loyal to Marion. She had a face you could chip a chisel on, but she had a heart of pure carbon steel. Twenty years before, her husband had run off with a cocktail waitress. Needing to support herself and her young daughter, Marion had become a cocktail waitress. I suppose you could make something out of that, some deep pyschological insight or witty irony, but I wouldn't advise it within earshot of her. When somebody got out of line at the Blue Parrot, a thing not unknown to happen, Marion did the bouncing, not me. Working evenings kept it to a minimum, but she dated men, even though she claimed not to have much use for them.

"Men are only good for one thing, " she told me once, "And they're not very good at that."

For women who have always been pretty, flirting isn't a head game but a deep, almost unconscious reflex. They learn very young that certain expressions and tones of voice, and later the subtle languages of stance, will get results a lot quicker than argument. Marion flirted habitually and good-naturedly with everyone, even me, though it was different with me being almost young enough to be her son if she'd gotten off to a quick start. Mostly she treated me like a precocious younger brother she suspected of peeking at her in the shower.

In a way, I was sorry when Lisa started coming around because Marion's banter got a rough edge to it, like a blunt knife, and any cook or bartender knows you're more likely to get cut with a dull blade than a sharp one. We'd had some good talks and good times, Marion and I, like the night we decided that if you drank enough of any kind of liquor you'd be able to speak the language of its country of origin. If you drank enough scotch, you'd develop a brogue. If you drank enough rum, you'd start talking Rasta. If you drank enough gin, you could speak Dutch. Etcetera. The science might be shaky, but for fun it beat hell out of Berlitz.

Neither of us believed in love, but we both believed in vodka. She cut hers with tonic water, that bittersweet quinine water no one but malarial ex-servicemen has any excuse to drink. Neither of us had managed to speak Russian, though I thought I'd come close a few times.

I didn't see why I should turn especially cool to Lisa just because Marion had a wild hair up her ass about her. I was cool to everyone on principle, drifting my glass canoe on my own private glacial lake and admiring the lack of scenery, just passing through. Sooner or later, somebody would make the owners of the old hotel the offer they were waiting for. Whatever happened, I'd be gliding along and a good canoeist dips his paddle without leaving a ripple.

In due course, I got Lisa's story. I knew that was inevitable when she came in the second time. You get a feel for the ones who are going to talk. They drink in quieter joints, where you can hear their troubles over the sound system. They sit at the bar or near it and they're a little too nice to the bartender. They're buying booze, not company, but they know it's hard to be rude to someone who's giving you money, even if it's not your own. If they're really on the skids, they're apologetic. They tell you every drink is the last one and they mean it, right up to Last Call.

At first Lisa couldn't stop telling me how much she liked The Blue Parrot. "It's such a nice cosy little bar," she said, "I mean, the beer parlour is so loud and tough, but it's so quiet and friendly in here and they're both in this weird old hotel. I mean, God, does anybody really stay here?"

"I really stay here."

That was true. I really stayed there, though not many other people did except for deadbeats and a few old fossils who hardly ever went farther from the place than a cab ride to the doctor's office or the bingo hall and mostly stayed in their rooms, quietly turning to stone.

My room, at staff rate, was directly above The Blue Parrot lounge. Not the Presidential Suite, but it had it's points. It cut down the travel time to work, for one thing. I could usually manage to negotiate one long narrow flight of stairs on schedule. On the other hand, coming up with an excuse for being late for my shift was a real challenge.

My room was interesting in its way, being taller than it was wide. Cleared of the old iron double bed, sprung chair I never sat in and chest of drawers that held everything I owned in the top one, it might have measured ten by twelve, but it had a fifteen foot ceiling. One of the tall arched windows gave me a narrow vertical casement view of the waterfront and a lot of sky. I'm not quite tall enough to inconvenience an undertaker, but the total effect of the room sometimes made me feel like I was shrinking.

The walls had been painted a colour that was probably green around 1920 when the hotel was built. When I moved in, I thought it needed cheering up, so I went around the corner to the second-hand store on Lonsdale and, for a couple of bucks, picked up a large map of the world and big poster of illustrated hands demonstrating the alphabet in the manual sign language of the deaf and dumb.

The map was comfortably out of date. Most of the colonies and more than a few countries no longer existed. Cities and towns were still in the same places, the cross-roads and watering-holes, way-stations and market-places, the entrances and exits where human beings have always congregated to make a buck off those who are passing through on their way to somewhere else, but many of the names had changed, some more than once, so there was no point in trying to match them up with the datelines in newspapers. It was a map of a vanished world I could contemplate with equanimity.

The poster was comforting, too. The reconciliation of gesture and language in those mute manual signals was an advertisement for silence. One night, as I lay on my saggy rented bed, I found myself wondering how lonely people who couldn't talk talked to themselves, but I didn't lose sleep over it. Stoli saw to that.

Lisa only half-believed me when I told her I lived there.

"I could offer to show it to you," I said, "But you've heard that before."

She nodded sadly. "I've heard that before."

She was the kind of woman who would have heard them all before. She must've been getting to me though, even then, because it was about that time I suggested to Fred, the Manager, that we start stocking a little better brand of white wine in The Blue Parrot lounge.

Heaving his bald sweaty bulk around a fresh keg of discounted nearly expired beer in the subdued pandemonium of the beer parlour, he looked at me like I'd just recommended a round of drinks on the house. When I failed to display any further symptoms of radical brain-fade, he screamed patiently, "Look, the Prince of Wales had a glass of wine here in nineteen-twentysomething. Soon as he drops by again, we'll upgrade the porch-climber. Okay?"

I nodded, wondering why I'd brought it up. Marion's intuition turned out to be a lot better than mine.

Chapter 3

Marion and I weren't the only ones who noticed Lisa was becoming a regular at The Blue Parrot. Most of the other two dozen faces and a few of the residents who frequented the bar, mainly Old Al and The Aunts, put their two cents' worth in. Two cents won't buy bubblegum anymore, but it's still the going rate for an opinion and it's comforting to know there's still one commodity that's impervious to inflation. What surprised me, since Lisa wasn't exactly The Blue Parrot type, was that the word, apart from Marion's catty hissing, was pretty favourable.

The Aunts were three old ducks who lived in three consecutive rooms on the third floor. Privately I thought of them as The Weird Sisters, though they were only friends who went everywhere together. Everywhere meant shopping and to bingo and crib nights at the Kiwanis Hall and, of course, to the old Lillooet Road Cemetery to visit the graves of their dear departed spouses. In fact, one of the old girls had hers cremated, his ashes enshrined in a small bronze urn on the night table beside her bed, a piece of foresight she never missed an opportunity to point out to the others on the occasion of those expeditons. She went along with them anyway, she said, because it was so peaceful there in the fresh air among the flowers and the wonderfully green grass.

As old friends will, they disagreed about everything, bickering ceaselessly about who had the most poverty-stricken, deprived girlhood, the most angelic mother, the most total ignorance of things sexual on her wedding night and whose insensitive and improvident husband had gambled, whored and drunk himself to death in the most tragic fashion after breaking the hearts of the family she struggled so hard to hold together.

Because they were three, it was impossible that they would ever agree about anything. No matter what the subject, it would always end with two against one, though I noticed it was never consistently the same two against the same one. The temporarily outnumbered would defer to the majority in that unquietly martyred way old women have, knowing her turn would come around. So their friendship endured, reminding me of the three blind women of ancient Greece who shared one eye between them.

Usually these debates were held in a corner booth of the Blue Parrot, where they paused to take a stirrup-cup of cheap Canadian sherry or port before their outings. This gave them an opportunity to differ about where they should go first, who had paid for the cab last time and who should pay this time, whether they should take port or sherry this afternoon, who had paid for the drinks last time, etcetera, and who should rummage in her enormous bag to produce, from a tiny change purse, my tip of exactly twenty-five cents.

Marion wouldn't wait on them if she could duck it. They drove her crazy, keeping her standing there while they told her she wore too much makeup, her high heels would ruin her feet, and to beware of fast men. Marion said they reminded her of her mother and it was bad enough being a mother herself without having to listen to it, times three.

The Aunts were forever knitting, turning out endless sweaters, scarves, toques and mittens for a legion of distant relations, none of whom ever came to visit them at the old hotel. They carried huge knitting bags with them everywhere and added on a few rows here and there as they waited in doctors' offices, backseats of taxis and while they played a dozen cards at bingo. Though they couldn't knit in the Blue Parrot because it was too dark, I modelled in the better lit dingy foyer as a tailor's dummy for the sleeves and waist lengths of uncounted nephews, grandchildren and great-grandchildren. It made me feel like one of the family — a kind of cable-stitched Everyman.

The most superficial interest in these woolly projects was rewarded with a genealogical exegesis of the intended wearer that would boggle The College of Arms, confound The Almanach de Gotha and make the Books of Leviticus and Numbers clip along like a Readers Digest Condensed Version. The Aunts approved of Lisa because she was willing to be consulted about appropriately fashionable styles and colours for the invisible recipients of their textile production. "They're sweet," Lisa said when I kidded her about it.

"They're three pains in the ass," Marion kicked in when she heard that.

I nodded, agreeing with them both, but even Marion was on side with The Weird Sisters when they declared that if a young woman had trouble, it must be on account of some man. Who was I to disagree with three generations of suffering womanhood? Especially on an afternoon when they were all looking at me sideways, as if challenging me not to be like all the rest?

There seemed to be an unspoken assumption that Lisa kept coming back to The Blue Parrot for some reason other than the quality of the house wine. I'd tried a sip once, just to see what I was pouring her, and it took three ounces of vodka to get the taste out of my mouth. From his perch by the wall at the far end of the bar, Old Al got in the habit of saying, "Here comes your girlfriend," every time she came in.

"I notice you stay for one past your limit every time she's at the bar," I retorted smugly.

Old Al just winked and said, "I'm old, son, but I'm not dead."

Everybody called him 'Old' Al. The adjective stuck to him like some kind of third personal pronoun. Nobody, least of all himself, could say how old he was, though according to him the Ark would have foundered if he hadn't been there to give Noah a few lessons in smart seamanship. In Old Al's book, the Flood was God's judgement on landlubbers, proof that no matter how high you climbed the waters could still rise over your head. But if you were at sea on a tight ship with everything Bristol fashion and knew how to shoot the sun and stars and box a compass, nothing, not even the Wrath of God, could drive you under.

"That's why being beached like this makes me bilious," he said.

Old Al would never admit to being a more or less permanent resident of the old hotel, though he'd lived there for years. As he told it, he was temporarily beached, that was all, and he talked constantly of 'getting a berth'. Up and out at dawn, he spent his days haunting the waterfront, eluding security guards, pestering Pursers and badgering Bosuns, conning Captains, trying to get taken on a crew.

Time and the times were against him. Ships had been getting bigger for decades, but the crews of those automated, computer-navigated barges were getting smaller. His opinion of modern mariners placed them below sea-level.

"Scow jockeys," he would mutter, shaking a gnarled fist at the huge container ships anchored in the Inlet as he turned into The Blue Parrot at the end of another wasted day.

No ship is allowed to carry crew or passengers over sixty years old without a doctor aboard, so even though Old Al's age was technically a mystery, a glance at his Seamans Discharge Book was enough to maroon him squarely on the beach at the old waterfront hotel. That weatherbeaten document was almost as thick as a volume of Lloyd's Register of Shipping and the early entries dated from The Age of Sail.

He spent his spare time visiting his doctor and extorting useless written testimonials to the effect that Old Al was still fit for sea duty from the poor man, who was getting ready for retirement himself.

"I'll bury that quack, no fear, my boyo," he told me with grim satisfaction over his glass of neat Demerarra rum, to which he added just a drop of water. "Mustn't drown it," he said, as if that was the worst thing you could do and , to a sailor, I suppose it is. He returned to the subject of his doctor, shaking his hawk-faced head sadly,

"Man's been sittin' on his arse all his life, like some fat damn barnacle. Now the tide's goin' out and he's high and dry. Got the empheseyma, arthritis, sciatica, cataracts, I don't know what all else. Comes from spendin' all your time around sick people, I expect."

I don't imagine he believed that, anymore than he truly believed that sea-time somehow wasn't included in your threescore and ten, but I never got tired of listening to his scuttlebutt. Unlike a lot of old men, he'd not only lived long enough, but well enough that he seldom repeated a tale.

I suspected the real reason he wanted to get to sea again was so he could die there, where he had lived. It was the kind of thing we talked around, not about, but I could see his point. People used to believe the souls of men lost at sea could never rest, not having had the blessing of relatives making the most of a last chance to throw dirt in your face or put their spare change on your eyes or tongue to bribe the ferryman, but I couldn't imagine Old Al's spirit being any less restless in the next world than it had been in this. I figured a guy who looked old enough to have been cabin boy on the Argo and Bosun for Chris Columbus was bound to wind up First Mate on The Flying Dutchman anyway.

Old Al referred to Lisa as "a tight-rigged little hooker", a description she surprised me by taking without offense, as though she instinctively understood it was a lot more complimentary in the old man's lexicon than in current usage. Maybe I gave her too much credit. It was impossible to mistake his meaning, really. As a result of who knew how many years experience with people from every continent and culture, he'd acquired that natural grace and courtliness royalty born and bred can only imitate.

"If things were different, son, I'd put a shot across her bows myself," he told me once, nipping at his rum.

"You mean, if you were a few years younger?" I asked stupidly.

"I meant, if she was a few years younger," he twinkled, giving me a light broadside raking.

I didn't let him calling Lisa my girlfriend go to my head. I knew perfectly well Lisa was using me, but I admired the way she finessed it. Most of the regular sports in their Saturday night drinking jackets took a shot at picking her up with varying degrees of subtlety and an identical lack of success. Like I said, she was a woman who'd heard most of the hopeless, hopeful openers men come out with more than once before. Still, she handled them gently, somehow managing to make each rejected aspirant for her favours feel like he'd paid her a unique and special compliment she'd be only too happy to accept, but for circumstances too personal and painful to mention.

I was a big help, of course. Since Lisa always sat at or very near the bar, these masculine manouevres had to be carried out in the presence of another man, which puts most guys off stride. Not only that, but in this case the man was The Man, the Management. I wasn't just some geek they were trying to cut her loose from. I was the man who poured or declined to pour the drinks, the man who could cut your table off, have you bounced or barred from The Blue Parrot for a day, week, month, year or lifetime. Like the owners of the old hotel, I was winning and I didn't have to do Thing One, which made a nice change.

In the prefabricated jungle darkness of The Blue Parrot, Lisa still apparently felt like a lost explorer who'd stumbled on another of her kind living at some remote outstation in the urban wilderness. When we were alone at the bar, huddled like conspirators in a hideout, she still couldn't resist accusing me of having gone native, run off to join the Indians.

"What are you doing here?" she whispered.

"I'm drinking my way across Canada to raise money for hangover research," I snapped back, "Hangover is a crippling condition which afflicts millions of Canadians, young and old. I soaked my sore head in the Pacific a year ago, right down here on this waterfront, and my goal is to soak it in the Atlantic, probably after a brutal night of rum and choruses of 'I'se the B'ye' in St. John's, Newfoundland...I'm off to a bit of a slow start, but I accept that it will take time and I'm committed because it's a worthy cause..."

"You know what I mean," she hissed, "You don't belong

here."

It was the second time she'd patronized me by acting superior to The Blue Parrot, Marion, the regulars, Old Al and The Aunts, and I let her know I didn't like it any better this time, though I refrained from calling her a "low-rent bitch." But after all, I was a steady customer down at Geoff's Barber Shop and the Sunrise Cafe around the corner, bought my paper, my smokes and the odd lottery ticket at the Moodyville Market down the block. I thought I'd done a pretty fair job of belonging, at least as good as any of the fresh out of prison rounders who occasionally shacked at the old hotel for a few weeks or months.

"Look," I said, wearily, "Most people feel like they don't belong where they are. If they live in the country, they long for the bright lights of the Big Smoke. If they live in the city, they dream of moving to the country for the fresh air and peace and quiet. If they live in the East End, they aspire to move to the West End. If they live in Kitsilano, they want to move to Shaughnessy or the British Properties. If they're in Vancouver, they want to be in Toronto, New York, or Maui, or Palm Springs, or London, Paris or Rome. Maybe the reason they feel they don't belong anywhere is that they spend so much time wishing they were somewhere else."

"You never wish you were somewhere else?" she asked, looking me right in the eye.

I just grinned, "If wishes were Porsches, beggars would drive, the man said," I replied, setting up half a dozen rum and cokes on a signal from Marion out on the floor.

"You," Lisa said laughing, "Just when I think I'm talking to you for real, you come out with some cheap smart crack."

"That's his job," Marion shot in as she swept the drinks away.

She was right. It was my job. Like cab drivers, barbers, hairdressers, psychiatrists and priests, bartenders hear such an unending monotonous litany of human sadness, treachery, mendacity, loneliness and loss that most age into surly automatons who pour drinks on command and answer every comment, confidence or confession with a universally noncommittal grunt. The only practical alternative is to rehearse your repertoire of smart remarks for all occasions, belt up your baggy pants, stick an exploding cigar in your face and leave them spastic in the aisles. If you really listen, if you take it all to heart, you'll finish your shift one night and pour yourself a .38 calibre nightcap.

Besides, people who talk to bartenders want to do just that. They don't want or expect you to talk back. They don't want to know you have falling arches, varicose veins, delinquent children, big debts, a drinking problem, a cheating wife, bad dreams and a broken heart. I told Lisa as much.

"You're saying you just tell them what they want to hear?" she said, sipping her wine. I noticed she didn't include herself in the third person. I smiled and saluted her with my short cold glass.

"When somebody asks you to tell them what you really think," I said carefully, "Don't you always get the feeling that what they really mean is that they want you to tell them what they really want to hear?"

She laughed sadly. "Sometimes I think I'm losing it," she said, looking into her wine glass as if it was a mirror whose surface was marred.

"Why's that?"

"Because you're starting to make sense."

It was my turn to laugh.

Chapter 4

Listening was part of the job. It came with the territory, as they say, so listen I did. Lisa's trouble wasn't unique. It wasn't even special, except to her. Her trouble was life, specifically men. Marion and The Aunts had been right on that score.

Lisa was a North Vancouver girl who'd married her childhood sweetheart at eighteen, when they were suburban hippies who believed in the Love and Peace Millennium and better living through chemistry. Some of them are still around, mostly retreated to bush towns in the Interior or up the coast, the walking wounded of the Pepsi Generation.

Part of the romance of drugs in those days was that they were a clandestine faith, like Christianity under the Empire. The rituals were secret, intimate and evangelical. Drug dealers weren't mere pedlars, but prophets of the Microdot Messiah, persecuted and martyred for the faith. I'd flirted with the New Order myself, but over the years drifted back to organized religion, the Mother Church of alcohol whose altars are in every restaurant, hotel and neighbourhood pub. Under the sign of Pisces, with a pony of Aquarius on the side, I had become pontifex and priest, officiating at the rites and administering the sacraments. Like I said, I drank religiously.

Lisa's young husband was handsome. He was a poet. He was a musician. He was an artist. He was on acid most of the time. They moved into the basement suite of his parents' home after being married in Stanley Park amid flowers, incense, sitar music and the excruciating poetry of Khalil Gibran. I got the impression she'd been more than a little intimidated by her husband and his friends. They had been secret steadies at fifteen, but separated for a few years and when they met again, she told me, his hair was longer than hers, which she still back-combed. Naturally she was happy to find herself readily accepted by a group of people who were obviously going to Change The World. She was less impressed when one of them wandered from the perpetual party in their living room into the bedroom at four in the morning, told them not to stop making love because it was beautiful and sat down to explain the meaning of life and mescaline.

Terrified of appearing straight or uncool, she'd still expected marriage to make some difference in their lives. Next, she discovered that her husband, who dutifully left every morning for the job his father fixed for him in the shipyards, wasn't bringing home any money. His excuses were as bizarre as a schoolboy's. He had lost his cheque. They would issue a new one next week. The payroll office was on strike. He had cashed it and given the money to a needy family.

It turned out he'd only reported for work the first few days. After that, he kissed her goodbye after a sleepless night of passionate love-making and gone up to the pool hall, where he hung around until the Nowhere Coffee House opened after noon. He spent the rest of the day there, picking at someone's guitar and talking about Changing The World.

She left him for one of his friends, an aspiring Buddhist who had wealthy parents, so at least her standard of living improved. His European mother filled the fridge of their apartment with homemade frozen cabbage rolls, casseroles and delicacies which Lisa ate while he observed a strict regimen of expensive macrobiotic foods. He even worked for his father, but he was saving his money to go to Nepal.

Eventually he did go, but not before she left him for one of his friends, a weed-dealer who worked for the Ministry of Fisheries. He was away a lot on a boat up and down the coast, counting fish and dealing lids and keys to the communes springing up in the islands and inlets. She went with him once, but she hated boats. She was afraid of the ocean. While he was away on a trip, she moved in with one of his former room-mates, a mousey little singer in a rock band who, she admitted, had always worshipped her. She didn't tell me all this in so many words, of course, but I learned to speed-read between the lines of dialogue years ago. People who like to talk, or need to, always wind up telling you more than they mean to.

Without being too obvious, I fished for hints about the fates of her former lovers. A good tracker can tell a lot about an animal he's never even seen, just from the spoor it leaves. Her first husband finally did get a job — at the Nowhere Coffee House. When that and the Sixties folded and the world remained stubbornly unchanged, the Millenium on hold, he got work at the pool hall where, for all she knew, he still handed out balls and kept time on the tables.

After pontificating for years about the wisdom of insecurity, the Buddhist had returned from the Himalayas on the magic carpet of his father's American Express Gold Card without the meaning of life, having acquired instead an Asian intestinal parasite that took months of treatment to evict from his colon. He got a haircut and made a lot of money selling home insulation in the exploding south Vancouver suburbs.

After she left the dope dealer, he went on the nod one night in a shack up coast with a smouldering Thai stick in his mouth and was prematurely cremated. In the wake of her departure the singer's mild stutter became more severe, especially when he he was drunk or stoned, which was all of the time, and he was kicked out of the band he'd started just before they swung a big recording contract. Last she'd heard, he stopped speaking to anyone, a voluntary mute.

"Sometimes I think I'm a jinx," she told me, sadly pondering her wine. That was my cue to tell her it wasn't her fault all the men she loved turned out to be such total losers. That was what I told her, of course. It was the gallant thing to do, after all, and with my policy of non-intervention, I could afford to be gallant. It's always the cripple on the bus who gets up to give his seat to the old lady, isn't it?

Maybe I even wanted to believe it. Men always want to believe anything said by a beautiful woman, despite several thousand years of warnings on that score. Beauty is the load in the die, the shaved edge of the card, the drag that slows the roulette wheel of Fate. It somehow seems to deserve happiness. Maybe it's because happiness is supposed to confer beauty. The plainest bride is radiant on her wedding day and at the birth of a child. At least, that's what they say.

Lisa's second husband was a break with the past. A late bloomer, he was her science project, like she'd been for her first husband. He was an electrical engineer, divorced. While everyone else was talking about Changing The World, he was learning to do it. When Lisa met him, he was letting his hair grow and learning to play the guitar, trying to loosen up. She turned him on and tuned him in. She made him stop and smell the flowers. The trouble with stopping to smell the roses is that you sometimes get a noseful of manure.

She moved into his turn of the century house on Vancouver Island, renovated in brass and glass and local pottery. She took riding lessons, even sailing lessons, because he had a boat, though she never got over her dislike of the sea. They had a child, a son, when children came back into fashion. She dabbled at various part-time jobs, but was bored by the semi-rural small town life of the Island.

Her husband had his work, a senior job with B.C Hydro. He dreamed of circuits, power grids. Marriage was a junction box where currents met. He had re-wired the house himself. He'd have re-wired the whole neighbourhood, the town, the Island, if they'd let him. At work, he told her, the unions wouldn't let him touch a screwdriver. He could only point to diagrams while bonehead electricians, who would never understand real power, did the work.

The wiring of their house far exceeded the standards of the Building Code. There were smoke alarms in every room, their batteries renewed on schedule every year. It was the safest house on the Island. Lisa told me she used to sit up at night all alone, chain-smoking under one after another of the alarms, just to see if they would go off. She began to get urges to set secret fires.

Afraid she might hurt her son and husband, she left them and moved back to the mainland, to North Van, because it was familiar, she knew her way around, though she avoided looking up old friends. I didn't comment on that, since I've noticed that whenever somebody says "I don't want to hurt you..." that's a good time to check that your jock-strap is firmly in place.

Since coming back, she'd had a few jobs but she'd quit most of them, it seemed, because the boss or the foreman or co-workers kept hitting on her. Every attractive woman, as well as some who really put your willing suspension of disbelief to the test, experiences sexual harrassment on the job more than once. But when a woman makes a career out of it, you start to wonder about her social skills.

She'd had a lot of boyfriends. Like most beautiful women, she always knew a lot of men and had few female friends. It's not always their fault. Women find it irritating, watching husbands and escorts drool, fawn and walk into walls in the presence of other women and, like men, know better than to trust their own sex.

Lisa's last boyfriend turned out to be a real hitter and she was afraid he'd come back one night and try to break into the crummy dank little basement suite on East First where she lived. She didn't have any girlfriends to move in with and she couldn't afford anything better. The solution to her problem was obvious. I didn't expect her to be alone for long.

In spite of it all, she insisted she didn't want another man in her life. She wanted to get custody of her kid, or partial custody at least, but her pogey was running out, she couldn't find a job and it looked like she'd have to go to Welfare .

"That's all I need," she said, "Having to report to the Ministry of Inhuman Resources every time I buy a lipstick."

I nodded sympathetically. I'd figured she had money problems from the way she discreetly checked her purse every time before she ordered her last glass of wine.

"Anyone who says money can't buy happiness doesn't know how to shop," I reminded her, but it barely got a laugh.

On top of everything, her landlord had started hassling her. We had a cold rainy spring that year and one wet night she'd taken in a cat that mewed at her door, dried him off and given him a bowl of warm milk. The cat was filthy and torn up from fighting the raccoons and feral cats who live in the lower North Van alleys. He stayed. He even let her bathe him and put a flea collar on him.

Her landlord lived upstairs and said he didn't allow pets, but he might be willing to make an exception for her, if she made it worth his while. He even offered to lower her rent, if she was agreeable. She told him to go fuck his hand and the cat hissed at him. So now she was going to be evicted and he'd threatened to whack the cat with a tire-iron.

I'd noticed she was carrying a big woven bag instead of her usual leather shoulder purse. I thought I'd seen it move once or twice, but I figured I'd just been over-pouring my own drinks.

"Don't let the cat out of the bag," I said, in a limp attempt at wit.

"I couldn't just leave him there," she said helplessly, "That bastard has a key to my place. I know he comes in when I'm not there. I think he plays around with my things, you know? Some of my panties have gone missing."

I didn't know what to do, but Marion did. She eavesdropped on most of Lisa's stories in cynical silence, but somehow the cat made them sisters, united in defense of helpless creatures everywhere. She demanded the bag, took it behind the bar, emptied my salt-rim dish down the sink and filled it with cream from the fridge, murmuring to the cat in a soft sweet voice I'd never heard before.

"Marion?" I ventured, "The health regs...Fred..."

"You let me handle Fred," she snapped, "And the slimeball Health Inspector who signs off on permits but hasn't stuck her head in the door, never mind a toilet, for five years."

I backed off while Lisa and Marion got their heads together over my bar, watching the little black and white cat lap cream and whispering about the everlasting perfidy of my sex.

I tipped another shot of vodka into my glass and laced it with water. I didn't understand what was happening. I wasn't sure I wanted to. After all, why fuck up a perfect record?

Chapter 5

Lisa called the cat Felix. It suited well enough, since he was pitch black, except for a neat patch of white around his eyes and muzzle which made him look like he was wearing a mask and added another dimension to his natural feline inscrutability. You have to be careful what you call things. Names resonate. Lisa might only have been thinking of the cat from the old cartoons, but I recalled from somewhere that his name meant "happy" or "fortunate" in Latin. A loose colloquial translation would be "Lucky," I guess, though from what I could see I'd've been inclined to call him Jinx. Felix didn't like to be touched, except by Lisa, but he let me run a hand over him once with an air of condescension that would've done a panther in a petting-zoo proud. I felt thin hard ridges of scar crisscrossed behind his ears and down his back. Though I suspected it was not the only one he'd ever had, he actually answered to his name, but only when Lisa said it. He'd pause in mid-stride, look at her, lower his head and give one loud brief purr, almost like the cough of a lion in the jungle night.

There are a lot of wild cats in the area. People move into the seedy apartments, rundown duplexes and Black Hole basement suites above the waterfront, stay until they can find or afford something better, then move on. Sometimes they abandon their cats and sometimes the cats, who are naturally territorial, abandon them for the bindweed-lined alleys, railway tracks and docks, alive with rats and pigeons fattened on spilled grain from the wheat pools, and the company of their own kind.

Years ago, when I worked on the docks at night one summer, I learned to be wary of the feral cats who hunted among the sheds and shops like embodied shadows. They were shyer and more dangerous than the family groups of raccoons whose turf they shared. The coons, Dad, Mom and the kids, crossing the yards with their queer hunched waddle, were a picture of domesticity compared to the solitary slinking cats.

I'd watched a pair of longshoremen who'd had too many nips from the ever-present bottle in the checker's shack tangle with one of those cats in the general cargo shed once. It was a long slow rainy afternoon shift and they were half-snapped making time and a half and they started tormenting this cat with long pike poles used by the tie-up crews to retrieve ships' hawsers from the harbour tugs. When they finally cornered the cat, there was a lot of hissing and spitting, followed by an inhuman scream. Then there were a lot more screams that were distinctly human.

One of the stevedores was nearly blinded when the cat landed on his head and gave him the works with the back claws. The wounds turned septic almost immediately and he has a set of scars that might win a beauty prize among some primitive tribe. The other one just wore long sleeve shirts all the time after, like a shy junkie. They both took a lot of stitches and a pin-cushion complement of needles, including the painful stomach shot for rabies. As far as I could tell in the confusion, the cat got away without a scratch.

You could tell at a glance that Felix's shyness had nothing to do with timidity. It was the shyness of a wild thing, which always seems like pride. In spite of it, he became a kind of mascot at The Blue Parrot. Mostly he stayed behind the bar with me or in Lisa's bag, but he'd pop out when somebody, usually Old Al, brought him one of the rank hot dogs sold in the beer parlour. The Aunts even knitted a small blanket out of multicoloured ends of balls of wool for him to sleep on. The regulars quickly got into the habit of buying him drinks. Naturally he favoured cream drinks, Baileys Irish Cream and such, but his favourite poison was a big shot of Tia Maria or Kahlua stirred into a wide-mouth old fashioned glass filled with fresh cream. No ice.

He lapped it up and sometimes he got a noseful. When he passed his limit, he'd slip around the bar, invisible on the floor of the gradually darkening lounge, and slide into Lisa's bag where he'd curl up and sack out, purring like a small outboard, faintly audible on quiet nights. He never staggered, which is saying something because he had two more feet to stumble with than most of the customers. He never got out of line either, which really is more than I can say for some of the two-legged variety. We only had that kind of trouble with him once and that wasn't his fault. A drunk American Navy boy who was trying to ingratiate himself with Lisa made the mistake of picking Felix up while he was trying to scoot into her bag to sleep off the effects my generosity. The swabbie caught the cat under the shoulders and lifted him up to his face, all the time making these patronizing baby-talk noises, "Nice kitty, kitty,..."

I never saw a cat less kitty in my life. Felix's forelegs lashed out and I held my breath, knowing whatever domesticated inhibitions he may have possessed had been thoroughly dissolved in cheap creme de cacao. Felix didn't scratch. Instead, with just the tips of his extended claws, he delicately caught the soft skin over the sailor's temples, before the hairline and right behind the eyes. If the guy had flinched, Felix would have torn off his eyelids. The sailor froze, suddenly sober, and I heard him whisper "Jesus and Mary..." as he contemplated the maritime career options of someone nicknamed Blind Pew.

Like I said, it was dark in The Blue Parrot and Felix always looked like he was wearing a mask, but I'd swear that for just a moment that cat smiled, showing a mouthful of needle-sharp teeth. Lisa spoke to him softly and asked the young man to put him down. As soon as his back legs touched the table and the frightened fellow released his shoulders, Felix retracted his formidable razors without leaving more than eight faint pink marks. With an arrogant lash of his tail, which nearly upset Lisa's glass of wine, he vanished into the bag so suddenly that a puff of sulphurous smoke wouldn't have been out of order.

If Lisa's lecherous landlord was going to kill that cat, I reflected, he'd better get him with the first swing. Otherwise, my money was on Felix.

Something had to be done before it came to that. At least I thought so, not that it was any of my business, but it was on my mind the night Pat came in. I hadn't seen him for a while.

"Been sitting on my ass gettin' pissed in Port Hardy, for lack of anything better to do," he told me, "Whacked my prop hard on a low-floater in Johnstone Straight and had to lay up gettin' the damn thing hammered out. Bent the shaft, too, of course."

Pat had been a fisherman all his life until the goddamn Wall Of Death bottom-dragging Japanese and the goddamn Russian and Polish factory fleets and the goddamn poaching Americans and the goddamn prickless eunuch Canadian Government made it just about impossible for a man to make a living at it. I liked Pat. He was fifty-six and made no secret of it, though he was in good enough shape to have dropped a decade without getting an argument from the ladies. He usually wore plaid shirts and baggy dungarees held up by Police suspenders. On special evenings at The Blue Parrot he wore an ageless Harris tweed and a tie that had been fashionable in the Fifties. On those nights, I was grateful for the low lights that had me stumbling to tables as I served drinks.

Pat never combed his thinning hair over the sunburned clearing on the top of his head. He didn't wear cheap white shoes or cologne designed for twenty-year olds with jock itch. Strictly an Old Spice and Aqua Velva man. He still kept a licensed boat down at the Mosquito Creek Marina, two blocks from the old hotel, and fished every season, "just to give the fish something to laugh at," he told me.

His wife had divorced him years ago, but he didn't hold a grudge. He admitted fishermen were hard to live with. Half the year they were off in a heaving green world of fish and whiskey or carousing with cronies in flea-shit towns up coast. Then they'd stomp in, stinking of fish, sweat and booze, dump a load of laundry full of scales like flakes of mother of pearl, toss a thick wad of bills on the table, fill out their pogey claim forms and spend the rest of the year sucking up rye-and-Seven in front of the tv.

I fixed Pat his usual; rye-and-Seven, no ice. He bought me one and I poured a little refrigerated Polish potato vodka, listening to the cubes crackle softly in the liquid, like a distant river breaking up in spring. I was expecting Lisa and it occurred to me that though they were both steady customers, they'd never met. Just to make conversation, I started telling Pat about her and Felix.

Maybe I was sticking my oar in. Not that I was trying to match them up or anything, but Pat had hinted to me a couple of times that he didn't like leaving his house empty while he was out on the boat. The increasing development and growing population of the North Shore meant that crime, particularly break-ins, was on the up as well.

It was a nice little house up on East Fourth. He'd done most of the renovations himself. He was good with his hands. We were good enough friends that I'd done some drinking there after hours. I'd take a bottle from the pool at work and replace it the next day or pick up a jug at Jack the Bootlegger's on First and Pat and I would drink quietly until dawn. He liked to drink and held it well, never turned argumentative, black or sour.

It would've been easy to take him up on his offer of the spare bedroom, but somehow I never did. I just didn't like living in other people's houses. It probably goes back to when my ex-wife and I were having one of our final skirmishes and she screamed, "Get out of MY house!"

Though I'd been paying the crippling mortgage, I suddenly realized I felt no more attachment to the place, the dry sauna, the hot tub, the vaulted Great Room, the microwave Jennair kitchen, than I would to a rented room in a cheap old hotel. Without intending to, she put herself on a par with one of those women you meet who invites you into a home some ex-something is paying the tariff on and there's that awful moment when she says, "Shhh..." and leaves you standing in the foyer while she pays off the baby-sitter and goes to check on the sleeping kid and you have to pee and you don't even know where the bathroom is.

So I left, feeling just the way you do in that situation, conspicuous at a suspicious hour in a strange neighbourhood, except that it was my own neighbourhood and when I finally flagged down a late-cruising cabbie, I didn't know where to tell him to take me.

I was doing fine in my peculiar tall room at the old hotel, but Lisa needed a place to live, a refuge, a man who would protect her without taking advantage of her situation. Under Pat's rough shirts and loud ties, I knew there was more old-fashioned gallantry and real gentleman than you'd find under most tuxedos these days. I'd worn a tux often enough to know.

At least Pat was willing to meet Lisa, so I bought him a drink and when she came in with Felix in the bag, his yellow eyes telepathically ordering a stiff Kahlua and cream, I introduced them. They chatted at the bar for a while, then sat at the nearest table, trying not to leave me out of the conversation completely. Once I was no longer needed to lubricate the discussion except in a purely professional capacity, I was perfectly happy to stay behind the bar and drink with Felix. Marion shot me a couple of looks that could've pinned me to the wall, but I didn't pay much attention.

Felix fixed things in the end. I think Lisa already liked Pat, or had sense enough to trust him on my say-so, but when Felix hit his personal wall he nipped around the bar, as usual, but instead of popping into the bag he sniffed Pat over tentatively, probably scenting ghost-salmon, then jumped into his lap and sacked out, purring like an engine on the redline. He'd never done that to anyone before.

By closing time, they'd settled on cooking and cleaning in exchange for room and board, no strings attached. Lisa was moving in the next day and I bought us all a drink on the house to seal the deal. Marion was the only one who wasn't impressed with my achievements in the field of diplomacy.

"Why couldn't you just mind your own fucking business?" she snapped, after they left.

I sighed hopelessly without answering. No matter how carefully you step, it's always on somebody's toes.

Chapter 6

I have to admit I asked myself the same question when I woke up with the sobering sun slicing through the tall window like a bright blade mercilessly finding the soft slit between the fourth and fifth rib.

The wonderful thing about being drunk — not kneewalking and slobbering on strangers drunk, but dispassionately, deliberately and decisively drunk — is that everything makes sense, even the things that don't. We'll do almost anything to get the feeling that things make sense — get up from a warm bed and go out into a cold world to a job we hate every day, get married, have children, plan holidays, join clubs and political parties, pay our bills on time, save for our retirement. If things still don't add up, some of us subscribe to Byzantine conspiracy theories involving the CIA, the Tri-Lateral Commission, the military-industrial complex, aliens in UFOs, Zionists, Freemasons and the Pope. Out of desperation, a few will join cults, become Moonies, Krishnas, born-again Christians or satanists. But most of us, in our lazy unimaginative way, opt for the handy remedy that's probably as old as civilization itself. We get drunk.

It usually works. It gets us through the crisis until the shrink-to-fit rationales we live by kick in again. But sometimes, the next morning, all the doubts and fears and questions return with the awful certainty of a hangover. Unwillingly awake, eyes unopened against the stab of light, sensing the presence of a headache that will be measured in megatons, you move your skull as gingerly as a truckload of old dynamite sweating in the sun, trying to figure out if what you did or said in an excess of inebriated understanding really makes as much sense as it did then. Or any sense at all.

"It seemed like a good idea at the time," is an all-time front runner on the list of Famous Last Words.

Why didn't I mind my own goddamn business? I guess because nobody ever does.

Anyway, Pat and Lisa were still on what was left of my mind a few days later when I ran into Pat at the barbershop. It was raining every night, but in the mornings the sun would burn through the clouds for a few hours. Squinting into it on the sidewalk outside The Blue Parrot was like staring at an acetylene torch. Clouds of white steam rose from the pavement and rooftops as the night rain evaporated. Everybody on the street had that slightly brain-damaged look they get on mornings when women can't manage the Maybelline and the men are too shaky to shave.

I wasn't surprised to find Pat in Geoff's barbershop. Geoff had been cutting hair at the same address, on the slope of Lonsdale where it dropped steeply down to the waterfront, for fifty-two years. With some customers, Geoff was on his third or fourth generation. My own father had brought me to Geoff to get my hair cut when I was too small to sit in the barberchair.

When I came to work at The Blue Parrot and live in the old hotel, I started going to Geoff's again, since it was just around the corner. Sitting in the chair, listening to the old-timers talk edited by the squeaky snips of Geoff's scissors, I could almost see my small serious six yearold face in the opposite mirror, raised to the height of manhood by the great padded board laid across the arms of the big chair, enthroned and robed in white linen stiffly gathered at the throat, like a boy-king or child lama at his investiture.

Geoff's was a real barbershop. When I was a kid, the window always displayed a couple of boxing posters, half-toned photographs of young men with their bulbous fists up, trying to look like world champions. Since the fight game faded on the West Coast, they'd been replaced by glossy bills for local opera and theatre productions, but Geoff's did not offer "unisex hair styling" and inside, it hadn't changed much.

Against the back wall, there was an old brown Warm-Morning oil heater. The walls were covered with framed caricatures by local wits and clippings from old newspapers, showing Geoff shearing neighbourhood celebrities, most of them now deceased. There was a novelty newspaper headline, also framed, proclaiming "Geoff's Barbershop Canada's Number One Happy Hour". The only new thing in the place was a huge slick Japanese colour tv set so the boys could catch the daily installment of their favourite afternoon soap, "One Life To Live."

The two chairs were now valuable antiques, all stove iron, porcelain and cracked and patched black leather. Geoff had a part-timer come in to help with the Friday and Saturday rush. Behind the chairs, a long enamelled counter supported an array of bottles reminscent of a bar, lilac water and Wildroot, hardly ever used anymore, peeking out from among rows of protein conditioners and ph balanced shampoos, Geoff's gesture to tonsorial modernity.

Against the opposite wall, a row of mismatched chairs flanked a coffee table where you could find the morning papers, reasonably current issues of *Field & Stream*, odd collectors' copies of old *Argosy* and *True* magazines, and a selection of *National Geographics* from the last four decades. If your taste ran that way, there were magazines devoted to less rare and exotic forms of natural beauty. Known as the Art Collection, they were kept in a drawer behind the second chair. Geoff still cut a lot of kids' hair.

I stuck my head in the door, said hi to the regulars, including Old Al, whose thin white mane Geoff always dallied over to avoid embarrassing him with a two-minute trim, and asked Geoff and Pat if they wanted coffee. They nodded.

"Just a small one," Geoff said, "My back teeth are floatin'"

The Sunrise Cafe shared Geoff's vestibule entrance. It was one of those places that offer Chinese and Canadian cuisine, a culinary tradition yet to be enshrined in any cookbook, but they could do bacon and eggs that wasn't completely afloat on a lake of grease. The restaurant, barbershop and the second hand store where I bought my map and the poster of the deaf and dumb alphabet were all one building and Geoff had owned it outright for years.

Developers had been to see him, of course. They'd offered him a lot of money for the old one-story woodframe firetrap. Geoff wouldn't say how much, but he let slip that when he turned them down they just offered him more. Like the regulars at The Blue Parrot, the old boys who hung around Geoff's, even though they didn't have enough hair between them to dull a razor, followed these negotiations with a mixture of fascination and fear.

"What'd you say then, Geoff?..."

"What'd you tell'em, Geoff?..."

Geoff would silence the angry buzz of his electric clippers with a throwaway flick of his wrist. "I told'em to go pound sand up their butts with a hammer. I'm seventy-four years old. I've been standing on this spot cutting hair for fifty-odd years, since I took over the business from my old man. I own the building. I got a house and a swimming pool and a lawn too big for me to cut. I got a twenty-foot Glasscraft down at the Marina if I want to go fishing. It's all paid off and I've got money in the bank. What the hell do I want with any more? When I kick, the kids get the lot and they can do what they want, but 'til then, I'll be standin' right here, cuttin' hair..."

A chorus of nervous cackled laughter filled the room.

"Good for you, Geoff!"

"That's the way to tell'em, Geoff!"

Geoff just laughed. "Besides, the old lady would go back on the rag if she had me underfoot every day after all these years..."

The meeting broke up as I handed Geoff and Pat their coffees. The old boys filed out to continue their aimless errands, to buy lottery tickets, pick up the Racing Form or duck into the Second Street liquor store for a pint of whiskey to tuck behind the paint thinner in the toolshed where the wife wouldn't find it and start going on about what the doctor said. Old Al was off to an appointment with his quack.

"Got to see how the poor bastard's arthritis is doin'" he

snickered.

When they were gone, Geoff gave a wink from above and behind Pat's nearly finished haircut. Pat caught it in the mirror.

"Take a little something to sweeten your coffee, boys?"

We both nodded.

"Wouldn't say no, Geoff."

"Still a bit of a chill in the mornings this spring."

From a drawer behind him, Geoff produced a mickey of Silk Tassel. Pat and I held our coffees out discreetly behind the chair while he topped them up.

"Knees up, Mother."

"First of the day."

I never drank rye except at Geoff's, where the caramel tang of the whisky rounded the edges off the slightly burned taste of the coffee. We never had more than one. Not that I was worried about Geoff getting sloppy and giving me a Van Gogh trim or anything. I never saw him drunk, except maybe once or twice at The Blue Parrot on his wedding anniversary or Armistice Day. A little mellow by closing time maybe, but never drunk.

The world is divided into people you drink with and people you have a drink with. Failure to observe this distinction can be embarrassing, expensive or fatal, depending on the company you keep. But there are times when one drink is a sacrament more binding than any number of soul-stripping midnight confessions over emptied bottles or weepy drunken couplings in the cold stale light of dawn. Being offered a snort by Geoff always made me feel like I'd been admitted into some unchartered and exclusive private club.

While we appreciated our coffee and Geoff finished off Pat's trim, I thumbed through a worn Geographic featuring pictures of the first manned moon landing. The moon was cold and arid in black and white. There weren't any signs proclaiming it Valuable Commercial Property, Future Site of Shopping Mall or Executive Townhomes. Not yet, anyway. It was only a matter of time. Somewhere, somebody is filling out a Development Permit Application or drawing up a subdivision plan.

Pat didn't bring it up so I had to.

"Lisa get moved alright?"

He nodded, risking Geoff's flying scissors.

"Yep. Took the pickup down and gave her a hand. Got it all in one load. Even the cat."

"Any trouble with the landlord?" I inquired blandly.

A smile slipped around the corner of Pat's mouth.

"He didn't want to refund her damage deposit. I had a little chat with him and he decided to be reasonable about it."

"I'll bet. You get things squared away at your end?"

Pat laughed softly as Geoff unwrapped him and brushed him down.

"You know women. Hadn't been there ten minutes before she noticed I'd been getting along without a dozen vital neccessities for years. I turned her loose with a shopping list and came in for a haircut I didn't need. Anything beats shopping, even Geoff's cheap rye."

We all laughed and drained our coffees. As I swung into the chair, Pat glanced out the door.

"Here she comes now. We're grabbing lunch next door, if you want to catch up."

Lisa stopped in the doorway with two bags in her arms and her face lit up like a kid at Christmas. Her fingers wagged at me from the bottom of one bag. She looked even better in the morning, with the slant of sun making a corona of the ends of her dark hair, than she did in the deepening shadows of The Blue Parrot. Pat took one of the bags, opened the door of the Sunrise Cafe and ushered her inside.

Geoff stared after them with his mouth slightly ajar, scissors poised above my left ear.

"Good thing you charge a flat rate instead of time," I said, "Or this'd be an expensive cut."

He started. "What? Oh. Yeah...I was just thinking. That's an awful lot of what makes life worth living to be walking around in one package."

It took about two minutes for him to work around to asking

and another two for me to explain about Pat and Lisa. I'm sure he'd already heard at least one version of the story. It'd been a couple of days, after all, and Geoff's barbershop was still one of the main exchanges on what remained of the old North Vancouver grapevine. There must be all sorts of new grapevines of discos and bistros because the suburbs are swollen with strangers, all the old big double lots have two houses crammed onto them and the patches of woods only kids could navigate are occupied by strip malls where kids practise pure electronic navigation on screens in video arcades. But there was a time when Geoff likely knew everybody worth knowing on the North Shore, directly or by reputation. Mind you, in those days, there were only a few places you could meet over a drink; The Blue Parrot and pub in the old hotel, the Eagles Club, the Legion and the Army & Navy Veterans Club, all within three blocks of Geoff's.

"I guess you've known Pat for quite awhile, eh Geoff?"

I don't know what I expected Geoff to tell me that I didn't already know. I'd liked Pat and trusted him from the minute I met him, but as a judge of character it wouldn't be the first time I'd displayed something less than the wisdom of Solomon. I guess I just wanted some reassurance that Pat wasn't likely to knock back too much of the secret formula one night and turn into Mr. Hyde.

"Shit, yes. Known him since he was a squirt. Cut his hair every two weeks since he could toddle, 'cept when he's out on the boat and when he was in Korea, of course."

"You mean the Korean War?"

Geoff nodded, considering my cowlick.

"Yep. With the UN peace-keeping force, back in '51. Not that old MacArthur did much of a job of keeping the peace. But Pat did his bit. Got himself wounded and decorated."

Never in any of our 3 am conversations had Pat mentioned the Army or Korea, never mind wounds and medals. I tried to imagine him charging into battle, a bayonet in his teeth, Thompson gun in one hand and grenade in the other, like a Sgt. Rock comic book cover.

"What'd he do? Capture Pork Chop Hill?"

Geoff shook his head, tidying my neckline. The clipper buzzed like a big angry hornet around my ear.

"The way I heard it, they were up near the Yalu River there, almost to China, freezing their butts off in the middle of winter, when the Red Chinese decided to mix in. The boys took a bad licking and the Chinese were moving fast, so a lot of them got caught behind the lines. Pat was one of them. Got hit in the shoulder, I think, but the guy he was with had bad schrapnel in both legs. Pat carried him fifteen miles on his back through the snow, until they got found by the Yanks."

"Jeeesus."

"Yeah," Geoff said, "Too bad. They got the guy to hospital, but they couldn't save his legs. Had to take'em both off. Later on, he got hold of a gun somehow and blew his brains out before they could ship him home."

"Shit," I said, "What a waste."

Geoff shrugged. "You can save some people from everything but themselves."

"I guess."

Geoff fussed with my part and loosened the wrap at the neck, but I was still curious.

"Did you know Pat's wife?"

"Yep. One of the Mason girls, from over the Boulevard way in those days."

"Pat says she found it pretty tough, living with a fisherman."

Geoff shrugged one shoulder. Because of the mirror on the opposite wall, we were able to talk face-to-face even though he was behind me.

"I don't know," he said, "I think everything was okay until the son got killed."

I watched my own eyebrows rise. I looked puzzled.

"But I've met Pat's son..."

Geoff nodded, shaking my stubble out of his clipper.

"That'd be the youngest, you mean. Richard, or Rick, I think they call him. I mean the older boy, Greg."

Pat had never mentioned another son to me. I couldn't recall even seeing an unexplained picture in his house.

"So what happened to Greg?" I asked, pressing him.

Geoff busied himself unwrapping my neck and brushing stray hair out of my collar as he spoke. I knew I'd still have to go back to my room and shower or my back would itch all day.

"It was pretty bad," he said, "Especially for Pat. That boy was the apple of his eye and the kid thought the sun shone out of his old man's forehead. He wanted to be a fisherman, just like his Dad. Probably would've been, though he was a bright kid and I think his Mom wanted him to go on to college. He couldn't wait to be old enough to start working summers on the boat. I guess he was about sixteen when Pat took him out...Pat was partners in a bigger boat then. Crew of four, I think, with the kid. Anyway, somewhere up near Stuart Island, I think it was, the weather turned real dirty. They were scrambling to get the nets in and somehow the kid went over the side...You know how it is on a workboat. You all try to keep an eye on each other. You're supposed to know where your watch-mate is all the time, but when the barometer drops and the shit hits, there's so much to do..."

"They never found him?"

"Oh, they found him. Days later, when the storm blew itself out and by then he couldn't tell them anything they didn't already know. They damn near lost the whole outfit staying out there looking for him, but it's just about impossible to see a man in the water when the sea's running high and it's bucketing down rain."

I tried to imagine it; the boat loaded to the hatchcovers, wallowing in angry gray swells, squalls of rain misting the wheelhouse windows, voices screaming themselves hoarse whipped away by the wind, howling in anguish and argument, with survival, the ultimate argument, finally winning, the craft cutting desperately for a sheltering cove.

"I'm amazed Pat ever went out again."

Geoff shrugged noncommittally. "Pat never said much about it. What could he do? Fishermen know the sea gives and takes away. It

48

could've been any of them..She took it hard, though. Next time he went out on the boat, she took the youngest and left. Maybe she was afraid he'd grow up wanting to be a fisherman, too. Maybe she just couldn't get over blaming Pat for losing Greg. You never really know with people, do you?"

I shook my head. "No, Geoff. You never do."

I paid for my haircut and tipped him about double the usual. He gave me an odd look and took it without thanking me. Slipping my jacket on, I stepped into the vestibule. Peering through the glass door of the cafe, I made out Pat and Lisa in one of the booths along the far wall. He was smiling indulgently while she rummaged in the bags beside her, gesticulating and talking to justify her purchases. I watched the dumb show, Pat examining the things she handed him with deliberately dubious looks, teasing her to more extravagant gestures and longer explanations, so he could enjoy the grace of her movements and the sound of her voice.

Deciding not to break up the party, I turned away and started back up the hill. In front of the second-hand store, a guy was hanging around, looking at the window display, a jumble of leftovers from other lives. He was around my age, but he could've used Geoff's help and his clothes were mismatched, the jacket too small and the pants dragging frayed dirty cuffs on the sidewalk. He looked like he was wearing someone else's shoes and had no place special to go in them.

In the window, another poster of hands demonstrating the signing alphabet of the deaf and dumb had replaced the one I'd bought. As he studied it, a rolled smoke smouldering in the corner of his mouth like a dud fuse, his dangling hands twitched in unconscious imitation of the illustrated signs. At the corner, I looked back and he'd moved on, drifting downhill with no motive more obvious than the force of gravity.

Chapter 7

The truce Felix had promoted between Marion and Lisa deteriorated into a cold war and Marion lost no opportunity to remind me that my supposed neutrality was highly suspect. I knew she'd gone out with Pat a couple of times, to movies or for Chinese food at the Jasmine Inn up the block. It was just for company, as far as I could see. She'd dated some of the other regulars a lot more often, even if she did claim not to have any use for them. Maybe she just didn't have any use for the ones who had any use for her. A lot of people have that problem.

I couldn't figure out what she had against Pat taking Lisa and Felix in, but I didn't lose a lot of sleep trying. Vodka saw to that and, besides, spring was showing signs of turning into summer, instead of detouring straight into autumn which is frequent enough to be usual in Vancouver.

I was getting out of my room more, taking long walks in the warm misty rain or aimless bus rides to strange parts of town. Even the stale air of the city tasted fresher and I felt taller, which made a nice change. There had been times in the middle of winter when I didn't leave the old hotel all week, spending the short gray days in my tall room, drinking and feeling like the Incredible Shrinking Man.

Pat and Lisa's arrangement seemed to be working out, too. He'd been on the brink of acquiring the irrevocable unselfconscious loneliness of the ageing bachelor who finally becomes so inured to his own greasy cooking and eccentric house-keeping that he can't remember a single good reason to change his habits. He needed someone to connect him to the inept, silly, glorious and tragic compromise of the social world again, or he might become one of those old men who sit in pubs, muttering contentious gibberish and ordering beers for an invisible friend in the chair across the table.

Lisa seemed much less downbeat, but in that cautious way of someone who's had a long run of bad luck and can't help feeling for the iron fingers in every velvet glove. They both still came into The Blue Parrot regularly, sometimes alone, but often together. They were good together, just easy, like an indulgent uncle and his favourite niece.

In the bar, Lisa could be gayer without seeming to be trying to attract male attention. Nobody was going to try hitting on her with Pat at her side. He was one of those men a young trout with a drink too many under his buckle could easily shrug off as just some old stiff, until his smart mouth earned him a closer inspection of those rope-and-hook scarred hands and muscles toned, not in some cute co-ed fitness centre, but by decades of brutal wet work on the unforgiving sea.

Sometimes Pat and Lisa brought Felix along, just for old times sake. Apparently he found his new home eminently satisfactory. Pat's neighbourhood was the oldest part of the North Shore, old enough that lanes still ran behind the houses, lined with garages, garbage cans, old cars, fruit trees and salmonberry thickets.

In his first week there, Felix had skinned every cat on the block, performed roadside rhinoplasty on every dog that carelessly mistook him for something to chase, and made a good start on the final solution to the mouse question in Pat's basement. Lisa jokingly accused me of turning Felix into a drunk.

"I feel so silly in the liquor store," she said, "I pick up a bottle of rye for Pat, my wine and a bottle of Kahlua for the damn cat. But if we have a drink without pouring him one, you should hear him growl. And when he kills a mouse, he brings it up and drops it right in front of the cupboard where the booze is and sits there growling until

I pour him a nip. You should see him try to catch mice after he's had a few. He ran smack into a wall the other day, trying to follow one down a hole."

"Look on the bright side," I said, "He doesn't drive, doesn't beat you and the cops don't bring him home every night."

I'd left them alone for a few weeks to get their domestic situation sorted out. Having put my oar in once, I decided three people couldn't paddle a canoe without the one in the middle doing some fancy twists and turns and I wasn't up to the emotional acrobatics. It would work out or it wouldn't. It was that simple. Most things in life are. We work hard to make them complicated, so we can feel some sense of achievement when things work out or have a good excuse when they don't. But the truth is that most of the great questions of life can be answered with a simple Yes or No.

Finally, one afternoon Pat stopped in for a quick one on the way home from working on the boat, but he really came to ask me why I didn't drop by the house for a snort anymore. I told him I was just letting the dust settle. He nodded understandingly.

"Lisa thought you might be pissed off at her or something," he said gruffly, as if the suggestion might embarrass us both.

"Why would I be pissed at her?"

He shrugged and shook his head. I shrugged and shook mine.

"Women," we said in unison.

"They get some strange ideas," Pat said.

"Don't we all?" I replied, "I'll bring a jug by after I close tonight, okay?"

"Already picked one up at the grog shop on the way here," Pat said.

We both grinned and bought each other one for the ditch.

See what I mean, though? I was just minding my own business, letting things take their natural course, like a river finding the mouth of a lake, and there Lisa was, imagining complications, inventing difficulties, assuming mysterious ulterior motives, when everything was really simple and clear to the point of transparency.

They say beautiful women are really insecure and maybe it's

true. Maybe Lisa needed to believe I'd really just stashed her with my friend Pat for future consideration, like a mountain lion caching his kill. Maybe she thought I was jealous of Pat for providing a haven I was unable to offer her. I don't know what she thought, any more than I knew why Marion disapproved so angrily of the innocent arrangement. The only thing I know for sure is that you never really know anybody until nothing they do is out of character.

When I got to Pat's that night, well after midnight, I knew the moment I stepped through the door it was a special evening. Not only had Pat bought a bottle of the Finnish vodka I liked and chilled it down in the freezer, Lisa had prepared a tray of thin spiced crackers, assorted cheeses, garlic sausages and pickles. The living room and the kitchen were spotless. She certainly seemed to be holding up her end of the deal.

Even Felix put in an appearance in my honour. Lisa told me he usually went out the window after dinner and came back just before dawn, tired from asserting his dominion over the nocturnal life of the neighbourhood, but he appeared as soon as I arrived, popping through the window like an animated fragment of the darkness outside, invading the kingdom of light. He meowed importunately at me.

"I'm off shift," I told him.

Pursing her lips in a smile, Lisa went to the kitchen to fix him his fortified milk. Pat took advantage of her brief absence to thank me for introducing them.

"I'd almost forgotten how nice it could be, just to have somebody around the house, somebody to come home to," he said, looking around his tidy home with slightly bewildered pride.

I nodded vaguely. Later, in the kitchen, while we were refilling our glasses, Lisa thanked me too.

"It's so great to be able to relax and snuggle down and really sleep at night now. I'd just about forgotten men could be kind and sweet and solid, like my Dad. You know?"

She looked so sad and happy all at once I almost hugged her. I think she knew, because she gave me a quick warm kiss before we went back into the living room.

It was a nice party—just four friends having a few drinks and later a delicious salmon Lisa stuffed and baked. Felix finished his first, sucked up the last of his drink and launched himself out the window to make his nocturnal rounds. Lisa excused herself and went to bed about three-thirty and Pat and I sat up over a long nightcap with only the kitchen light on and very soft innocuous jazz on the radio. He was quieter than usual, but I didn't mind. I knew there was contentment, not sadness, in his silence.

I'd missed drinking at Pat's place. An old wartime house, small but cosy, it was on the south side of Fourth, which meant the house faced north onto the street, but builders in those days stuck to the plans and put the living rooms at the front of house in spite of the spectacular views of the city and Inlet out back.

It was strange, but no stranger than building a room taller than it is wide, I guess. Over the years, Pat had gutted the place and reversed the plan, putting the living and dining rooms at the back, and added on a big sundeck. From his living room, Vancouver at night was a mirage of a fabulous city, suspended above the black Inlet, it's reflected colours wavering in the dark water like an image on a distant phantom lake.

I left down the alley just before the sun came up. It's not always darkest before the dawn. In fact, the sky turns from black to a suggestive blue, suffusing the silent suburban streets and dew-damp lawns with a mysterious, unreal luminescence. It's the signal for the small birds in the trees and alleys to start tentatively whistling themselves awake.

At the back gate, I stopped, breathing the cold-pressed dawn air. Feeling I was being watched, I looked up into the thick darkness of an old cherry tree. Hovering above a branch, like the disembodied face of the Cheshire Cat, was Felix's small white mask.

He meowed softly, once. I shrugged.

"I don't know, Felix. You tell me."

Chapter 8

After that, I hung out at Pat's more often. Summer was coming on fast and hot and we had a couple of early barbecues at the old brick pit in the back yard. Pat had built it himself out of scavenged bricks and flagstones years before when he had a wife and family, but it had fallen into the sad disrepair of disuse, like a deserted shrine. He spent a whole day fixing it up, clearing the drafts of leaves and wads of cobwebbing, removing the congealed greasy ashes of family cookouts in vanished summers, replacing the rusted iron grille with a bright grid of stainless steel.

I dropped in for lunch, early dinner or a nightcap a few times when Pat was out on the boat. That wasn't my idea or Lisa's. Before he took off on a trip, Pat himself had made a point of asking me to check on her. Somehow though, Lisa and I weren't as easy together as when he was there or when we occupied opposite sides of the bar.

When we were all at Pat's, she'd often give me a sisterly hug or kiss as I arrived or left. When we were alone we could still talk easily enough, but we both got a little stiff and nervous if we stood too near each other and we sidestepped to avoid brushing into each other in doorways or Pat's small kitchen.

Not that we were ever truly alone. Felix was always around in the daytime, treating the furniture like a suite of chaise longue, and if I made a late call he seemed to know I was coming. He would just appear suddenly and silently between my legs as I was about to knock on the front door, utter an imperious *maiow*, and the door would swing open on Lisa, smiling as I stood there with my arm upraised like a comical lawn statue of Diogenes whose lamp has been swiped by vandals.

The first time he did it, I nearly jumped off the porch, but I soon got used to it. It was just part of the thing between Felix and Lisa. He was a peculiarly communicative cat, which is to say he was flat out uncommunicative and indifferent most of the time, but when he wanted something even I got the message clear and loud.

Between Felix and Lisa that empathy approached telepathy. In the middle of talking to me or Pat, she'd get up, go to the kitchen and put out a snack or a drink for the invisible cat. A minute or two later, he would pop out of nowhere, as if he'd walked through a wall or risen out of the floor like a wisp of black smoke.

Lisa told me she sometimes woke in the night at odd hours without knowing why, not afraid, but with a funny feeling of something about to happen. Invariably, she said, Felix would drop through the open window onto her bed and crouch beside her head, purring out long tales of his adventures in the otherworld of darkness.

I chuckled at that, of course, and so did she as she told me, but there was no denying something weird about her and that cat. I noticed he never took his eyes off her, for one thing. If she left the room for a moment to go to the bathroom or kitchen, he didn't follow her, but watched the door steadily until she returned. He didn't exactly fawn on her. He never did that with anybody, but he would couch like a leopard or panther in long grass, willing himself to be unobtrusive to the point of invisibility, yet watching her all the time with a fierce fixed slit-eyed stare, as though hypnotized.

One night, when I'd had just enough vodka that the whole world was taking on that cool neutral transparency I liked, it struck me that it might be the other way around. For a moment, I had the uncanny notion that it was the cat who had hypnotized her. Sitting across from me on Pat's couch, her movements suddenly seemed jerky, as if controlled by invisible wires, and I couldn't understand what she was saying. I felt like Felix was trying to talk to me through her, trying to make her human tongue pronounce some ancient feline language of the dark.

I'd had a lot to drink, obviously. My grip on reality was a bit loose at the best of times, but that feeling was hard to shake. No matter how reluctant I was to entertain the idea, there was something about Lisa and Felix that made me think of a witch and her familiar.

There were other signs that could've told me things about Lisa if I hadn't been busy mulling over that kind of stuff. For one thing, Pat and I seemed to be her only friends. From time to time she made vague references to friends who we would doubtlessly like as much as she did. She would invite them over for dinner or a barbecue soon, she said, but not one of them ever materialized and after a while she stopped mentioning them. She was perfectly content, it seemed, with Pat and Felix and me.

"We're your Unholy Trinity," I told her one night when Pat was away and I was more than half in the bag, "Pat's the Father, which makes me The Idiot Son, and Felix is the Unholy Ghost."

That was the only time something almost happened between us. Pat was out on the boat, it was my night off, it was hot and Lisa invited me to come up and barbecue a salmon from the freezer. I acquitted myself like a man at the pit, surviving the suburban ordeal by fire by quickly surprising her with a bed of evenly glowing coals. When her praises became extravagant, I confessed to some previous experience with the tongs and toque, which opened up the whole question of my former life.

Frankly, I dislike people who are always going on about their ex-wives and ex-lives, probably because I hear so much of it across the bar, but that night I talked to Lisa about mine for the first time. At least, I covered the main points without going into forensic detail. I even told her about the child. She listened with an interest so rapt I was not surprised to learn it consisted mainly of relief.

"I was always a bit afraid of you," she confessed, after I finished, "Not really afraid, but, you know, you're always so cool and distant. I mean, you've been so kind to me, but I felt you were kind because you didn't really care one way or another and that made it easy for you."

She had me there, I had to admit. Callousness and cruelty don't automatically pair up. When you really don't give a shit, it's easier to be kind and considerate than not. In the long run it leads to less hassle and less strain. Sadism is the mark of a man who has an axe and too much time to grind it.

I was also aware that, to some extent at least, this confession of hers was a ploy. When a woman tells a man she is afraid of him, she flatters him, invests him with a certain roguish and romantic charm, while at the same time obligating him to titillate without terrorizing her. She makes him a kind of protector.

In the thickening twilight, Lisa and I were as close as could be without moving from our chairs. We were believers in large glasses. You didn't have to get up and go to the well as often and it kept your drink count low. With those big balloon goblets you can dust a bottle in three refills, but you can still say you've only had three glasses of wine.

For a while we laughed at Felix, trying to catch the midges and craneflies rising out of the grass. He'd wet his whiskers pretty heavily and wasn't having much luck, his jumps and swipes at the insubstantial insects ending in undignified flat-back pratfalls and disgruntled meows.

As the darkness became substantial, he settled into a crouch, a shadow within shadows. Lisa and I talked on for a long time and, like a lot of those kind of converstations, I'm not sure what about, exactly. I know at one point she talked about her little boy and cried, squeezing my hand tightly in the dark. She talked about Pat, too. About how much she missed him when he was out on the boat and worried about him, all alone out there on the ocean she feared and hated. When he was home, she said, she hadn't felt so safe and peaceful and happy since she was a kid.

Fear of large bodies of water is not unreasonable. Anyone who doesn't have a healthy respect for the ocean should move to the Prairies. But I've always found it a little odd to meet people who are positively phobic about natural phenomena; lightning, thunder, mountains or the sea. It's as if they can't deal with anything that isn't on a human scale, subject to human control and manipulation. Myself, I'm inclined to agree with the Japanese, who say there is no such thing as bad or good weather, there is only weather.

Nothing happened until we started cleaning up the plates, glasses and bottles and I was getting ready to leave. Lisa asked me to stick around until she had everything put away because she hadn't left any lights on and dark houses frightened her. That was a fear I could understand.

We were both suddenly quiet after so much drink and talk in the dark. Somehow, under the sundeck, in the deepest shadow where we fumbled the last of the leftovers into garbage cans, I found her in my arms, kissing me in a way that was anything but sisterly. The resilient warmth of her breasts spread through my chest and there was a stirring against my inseam in spite of the massive dose of anaesthetic I'd self-administered.

At the same moment, I was acutely aware of the dark empty house, Pat's house but still someone else's house, of the awkward single bed in her room and the lonely double in Pat's, the matrimonial bed, haunted by the ghosts of countless consummations. On the whole, I'd've preferred to just lie down in the cool neutral grass of the back yard. The neighbourhood was asleep. There was no moon. Even that arid observer of the night life of our planet was looking the other way.

It did occur to me to wonder, in a way, what we were doing. Or, at least, what Lisa was doing with me. She'd just been telling me how happy she was. It was as though somebody had been showing off a priceless Ming vase they'd finally acquired, then tossed it casually across the room, counting on you to catch.

It wasn't as if I'd never seen anything like it before. People devote their lives to the pursuit of happiness, but on those rare occasions when they achieve it, they generally can't find ways to fuck it up fast enough.

We were shocked out of our sensual stupor by the unearthly screams and snarls of a catfight that erupted in the back yard.

"God!...Wha'the hell!" we both spluttered, leaping apart and trembling in the total darkness. Evidently one of the local cats, unable to resist the smell of salmon wafting from the cooling barbecue, had tresspassed on Felix's turf and paid the price in fur and blood.

"Better put some lights on," I said.

The moment passed and Lisa seemed to sense it too. When she had the house lit, I didn't go in. We said goodnight at the basement door and I left through the back gate.

On the way, I passed Felix. His fur was still standing straight up on his arched back and he glared at me with huge yellow eyes as he perched on the brick barbecue, for all the world like a black imp from Hell scavenging a ruined altar for stray crumbs of the Host to be used in some unspeakable charm.

Chapter 9

When Lisa and I saw each other a few nights later back at The Blue Parrot, things were easier between us in a way. It was as if, having got sex out of the way somehow, we could try to really get to know one another. Whatever I'd told her that night, sitting in the dark in Pat's back yard, it was enough to make her feel entitled to know more.

Like most weeknights in The Blue Parrot, it was as lively as a morgue on Monday and after two glasses of wine Lisa casually asked me what kind of person my ex-wife was. Usually, when a woman asks a man about past wives or girlfriends it's to rate the competition, like watching the other team's films. I thought we'd got around that stage, but maybe she couldn't resist going through the emotional motions. I was at least one drink ahead of her, so I took my time adjusting the level of my glass, lowering it, then topping it up.

"You don't have to tell me if you don't want to," she said, making it plain I couldn't not tell her without implying I didn't trust her and hurting her feelings.

"She was perfect," I said, just to put things in perspective.

Lisa gave me the wide-eyed surprise double-take.

"Perfect?" she repeated incredulously.

I nodded. She thought about that for as long as it took to drink another ounce of her wine. "If she was so perfect," she said, trying hard not to sound defensive, "Why aren't you still with her?"

I was ready for that one.

"You try living with someone who always looks like the cover of Chatelaine, even first thing in the morning after a night on the tiles. Someone who would never be caught under-dressed or overdressed, whether she was gardening, selling real estate, or hostessing a live dissection. Someone who never sweats, let alone burps or farts, but always smells faintly of fine eau de cologne. Someone who always has a drink in her hand, but never gets drunk..."

"Sounds like Martha Stewart on bad drugs," Lisa murmured challengingly.

"She had the knack of making everyone she met feel like she knew exactly what they meant, no matter what coke or martini-induced grandiose babble they were spewing, and that it was the most exciting and insightful conversation she'd had all day. Naturally everyone thought she was wonderful and that she was absolutely right one hundred percent of the time."

Lisa nodded knowingly. "I get the idea..."

I smiled and topped off her wineglass, on the house.

"In a drifting lifeboat filled with survivors talking cannibalism and drawing lots, my wife would've magically produced a tray of canapes..."

She smiled and took one last shot in the dark. "There must've been something she wasn't perfect at...?"

I knew where she was going and shook my head. "Nope. In our relationship, I was the one who had to fake the orgasms."

She laughed and drank some more of her wine. After a minute or two, she asked, " Is that why you married her? Because she was perfect?"

"It was just like a fairy tale," I said, "One of those ones where you catch a fairy and it grants you a wish, but you get exactly what you wish for and it turns out to be not quite what you had in mind."

"Been there," she said, taking another sip of wine. How she could drink that stuff without gagging beat me and I took another swig of my own cold clear mixture to get the imaginary taste out of my mouth.

The Blue Parrot

"I read somewhere that when God wants to punish us, he answers our prayers," she said suddenly, "Do you believe in God?"

I shrugged. I didn't want to get into cocktail theology: all religions are One, Jesus'd make the Pope pawn his rings to feed the poor if he came back today, blah, blah.

"I'm not religious..." Lisa started to say.

"But you believe in Something? Right?" I cut in, laying the sarcastic emphasis on like an acid power-wash, "There are no atheists in detox wards. I know."

"I get it," Lisa said, backing out of that minefield, "You married your wife because she was perfect and she married you because you know everything."

"I asked for that," I laughed, acknowledging the bulls-eye. "But actually I think she married me because I fit into the plan."

"The plan?"

"The Plan," I said with a nod, "I mean, she was perfect, so she need a perfect husband. She could've hooked some corporate suit on the express to success, a chartered accountant or lawyer. Okay financially, but a bit dull, like pinstripe wallpaper. On the other hand, if she married some artist or actor or, God forbid, a writer, life would be interesting alright, if you're the kind of person who finds paranoia and poverty amusing. She isn't."

"The other night, you told me you were in advertising," Lisa reminded me. It was the only time she referred to the non-events of that evening.

"That's why I was perfect," I replied, "When we met, I was a lowly copy-writer, but she fired me with ambition to become a creative director and account executive. I was good at it. I made a lot of money and lots and lots of money for other people. We had to entertain a lot. Only people who were interesting or rich and people who are rich are always interesting, if only because you want to know how they came by all that money. My job was creative enough that she could one-up her friends and relatives, but not so creative she had to worry about me slicing off my ears and couriering them to call-girls or walking a pet lobster down our suburban crescent street."

"What kind of advertising did you do?"

I topped off my glass again. "When I left, my biggest accounts were the major brewers and distillers. Liquor ads."

Lisa barely stifled a giggle. "And now you're a bartender?" she said, mocking in spite of herself.

"One thing I've never suffered from is an irony deficiency."

I let her mull that over while I finished my drink. The vodka was numbingly cold and almost thick, like meltwater in spring. I was drinking too fast and talking too much, but it didn't matter. The better someone thinks they know you, the more perfect a stranger you become.

Slipping out from behind the bar, I nipped across the hall to the Gents for a cold water wash. Shoving my face in the brimming sink was like bobbing for ice-cubes, but it straightened me out. Soaking a paper towel in the freezing water, I slapped it across the back of my neck as I combed my hair. I got back just in time to toss up a couple of rye and cokes for Marion and a rum straight-up for Old Al, both of whom gave me pointedly curious looks.

Smiling benignly, I made myself a drink that was mostly water and drifted down the bar to where Lisa was still sitting. The interrogation wasn't over.

"So did you quit?...Or something?" she asked carefully. She was right the second time.

"I was too good at my job," I said, modestly raising my glass, "Demographically, as we used to say, I was part of my own target market. My own best customer. The eternally young, insufferably healthy, impossibly happy people in the beer and booze ads, where everyone's glass is always full, it's always the first drink and nobody looks like they even know what a hangover is."

"You had a drinking problem?"

"W.C. Fields used to say he didn't have a drinking problem as long as he could get a drink. I just spread myself too thin. You can't be a workaholic and an alcoholic. If you really want to succeed, you have to know how to prioritize."

"Your poor wife..."

"Yes," I said, "She had problems of her own and I wasn't there for her, as they say. After the baby was born, she got back into shape at one of those electric gyms that let you do everything from running to skiing in air-conditioned comfort and started dating other men."

"While you were still together? And with a new baby?" Lisa looked genuinely shocked.

"Kind of a radical cure for post-partum depression, you could say, but it wasn't that simple," I explained, "See, the baby was supposed to make us the perfect family. Perfect wife plus perfect husband times big incomes divided by dream home in the suburbs equals perfect child...Only the baby wasn't perfect."

"She wasn't?" Lisa said apprehensively. I'd told her I had a daughter, nothing more.

I made a fresh drink, a lot stronger this time. The first mouthful of lukewarm vodka stuck in the back of my throat like a medicine that's worse than the disease.

"Not long after she was born, we noticed she hardly ever made a sound and she didn't seem to react when you talked to her or even to loud noises. We thought she was just a really good baby at first, but we took her to a pediatrician and he confirmed it. She's deaf...And dumb," I added, just to drive the point home.

"Oh God..." Lisa looked ill.

"I guess it was natural for my wife to blame me. After all, she was perfect, right?" I said with a grin I knew wasn't quite making it. "You know, it's funny how things hit you. At the time, all I could think about was that she would never hear her own name. How is she ever going to figure out who she is, when she doesn't even know what her own name sounds like when somebody calls out to her, or says 'I love you', or whispers it in the dark?"

Lisa bit her lip. "What did you call her?" she asked.

I took a wicked hit from my glass, thinking about how you should never ask a question unless you're absolutely sure you want to hear the answer.

"Her name is Lisa," I said mercilessly.

That cut back on the backchat considerably. On the other hand, I couldn't shut up. I was on a roll.

"It was harder for my wife than for me. I couldn't stand it, being alone in the house with that beautiful little creature I just couldn't communicate with. But I had my work, so I started staying later and later at the office. After a while, even that didn't help. The numbers didn't make sense anymore."

"The numbers?"

"Yeah," I said, "We spent a lot of time and money on market research. Getting the numbers. It's supposed to tell you what people want, but the more I studied them, the longer I sat there in the office with a bottle of vodka and the phone off the hook, the more it seemed like the numbers were just telling us what we already knew, that we had already told people what to want and they were just running our own ad campaigns back at us..."

"What to want?..." Lisa looked puzzled.

I smiled and drained my glass, letting the ice chips rattle against my teeth, setting the residual nerves on edge.

"That's when it dawned on me that the source of most human unhappiness isn't not being able to get what they want, but not knowing what they want in the first place. I mean, all anybody really wants is to be happy and not to be afraid to die. But they don't want to know that you can't buy those things down at the mall, because it'd mean they were working and saving and paying their bills for nothing. They want to be told what to want, what to wear, what to drink, what to drive, what they can buy in the meantime that will make them forget how short and unfair life is and how unhappy and afraid they are."

I made myself another drink, even stronger this time. "Anyway," I continued, "The more I thought about it, the weirder it seemed to be in the business of telling people what to want when I didn't know what I wanted any better than any of them. I was just running my own bullshit back at myself and calling it demographics."

"It sounds to me like you got tired of living with the lies," Lisa said softly. I was supposed to be flattered, but the vodka had shorted out all those circuits, leaving only a pure lucid flow. I was transparent. I could see right through myself.

"That makes it sound noble, but it wasn't," I said, shaking my head. I'd had enough of those types sitting across the bar from me; the professional failures who point to their poverty as vindication, who advertise their cowardice as a kind of twisted courage, the three-drink idealists whose fervent belief in every lost cause, impossible scheme and unlikely plot masks a lack of faith in their fellow humans and the world that is grimmer to contemplate than any cynical pose.

"I was drunk all the time," I admitted flatly. "My work went to hell and the agency suggested I take some time off and consider my career options. My wife made it simpler. Shut up or ship out. I did both."

"And got a job as a bartender?"

I shook my head. "No, I knocked around a bit, visiting friends in Toronto and California who all wanted to introduce me to 'contacts', but I got tired of everyone feeling sorry for me, waiting for me to get it together and get out of their lives. People tend to avoid anyone having a bad run of luck. Even the best friends can't help being a bit afraid it might be contagious. After a year, I came back to town and hit up an old buddy for a job on a community newspaper."

"In advertising?"

I shook my head and drank. "As a reporter. I trained in journalism before I went into media writing. I figured I might as well find out how I liked it."

"I guess you didn't," she said, looking around. The thin crowd was getting slimmer by the minute. Old Al sat at the end of the bar like a patient buzzard. It was almost closing time. I killed my drink.

"Reporters drink even more than ad-men," I said, "But it's harder to tell lies and pretend they're the truth than it is to tell lies everybody knows are just lies to make them buy things."

"Oh," she said, looking into her empty glass.

"Yeah," I said. "I learned that before you decide you can't live with the lies, you better be damn sure you can live with the truth."

Lisa looked like she was thinking about something else.

"Last call for alcohol," I announced to no one in particular, replenishing my glass. Lisa declined.

"And you never see your little girl?" she asked.

"She lives with my ex-wife's mother in Burnaby. It's a bit awkward. She's almost six now. She goes to a special school for kids like her. I've seen her a few times, but it shakes her up. It's so hard for us to communicate. So maybe it's better I don't, for her sake..."

Lisa nodded sympathetically. At last we really had something in common, I thought, even if it was only the lies we told ourselves. Whenever we want to weasel out of doing something painful, it's always for someone else's sake.

She put her jacket on slowly as I built Marion's last order, but she hesitated at the bar, waiting for me to ask her to stay until I'd cleaned up and closed, giving me a last chance to change my mind about the other night, to admit I didn't want to be alone tonight, that I wanted her to stay with me and perform some futile ceremony of sensual magic against the dark.

There's no aphrodisiac like misery. Not only do women in trouble turn men into Knights Tumescent, but a man in pain seems to have a magic melting effect on the chilliest ice maiden. With men, the belief that a good fuck fixes everything never amounts to more than a hairy pose, but women have an absolute faith in their femininity to work miracles.

"You're a cab," I said, picking up the direct line to North Shore Taxi.

She nodded sadly and went out into the lobby as Old Al wheedled a last tot of rum out of me.

"Sure you can make the stairs, Al?" I inquired. He'd had a discouraging day on the docks and a couple past his limit.

"Been up steeper gangways than that and a lot drunker, my old son."

"Good," I said, "You can give me a leg up."

He nodded, looking at my glass. Apparently, he'd been keeping better track than I had.

"That I'll do, son," he growled, "That I'll do."

Chapter 10

I had the next day off, but I avoided going up to Pat's. I wasn't abandoning Lisa, but I knew Pat was due back any day and that last look she'd given me at closing time the night before had been almost irresistible. I was just glad that I'd been too drunk to make anything but a fool of myself.

That was a strange evening, because I usually don't get drunk behind the bar. The management feels it sets a bad example. I wondered how deliberately I'd done it. I wasn't surprised when I got Lisa's story, but I never thought she'd get so much of mine. Still, the easiest person in the world to outsmart is yourself.

Before the night of our last barbecue, when I'd let her glimpse the murky outline of my past, I'd never talked to anyone about anything that happened before I came to The Blue Parrot. Not talking about something doesn't mean you never have to think about it, but it helps. Talking about it changed things. When you talk about something, you feel like you have to do something about it or else join the bullshitters, the ones who spend their lives leaning on bars and coffee counters, sitting in old hotel lobbies or on bus benches, kneeling in confessionals or lying on psychiatrist's couches and talking, talking, talking.

So, on my day off I went for a bus ride. Nothing unusual about that, though a few years ago, when I was a successful advertising director, I thought public transport meant having to drive a car designed in Detroit. Only secretaries rode buses; slim secretaries reading fat historical lace-rippers and fat secretaries reading slim Harlequin romances.

What was unusual was that this time I had a destination. I'd made the phone call first thing, before I had a chance to open my eyes over a Bloody Mary and talk myself out of it. That was another unusual thing; I was as cold and sober as the summer rain that soaked my shoulders at the bus stop.

Usually my bus rides were eclectic detours, devious digressions and diversions I pulled off with minimal planning by letting chance and coincidence play Conductor. Hundreds of bus schedules with diagrammed routes and timetables graduated to the minute had been handed to me by the drivers and transit supervisors I had to ask for directions when I lost myself, wandering in some distant, familiar yet foreign suburban mall. I always accepted these little booklets with the automatic politeness of someone receiving a proffered religious tract.

As soon as I got on a bus pointed back in the general direction of the North Shore mountains, I'd tuck the pamphlet down the side of a seat and forget it. They were always out of date in a few weeks anyway and all those pages, with their ranks of tiny numbers marshalled like some progressive equation, were an answer to a question I didn't want to ask, the solution to a mystery I preferred to remain unsolved.

Besides, I was never really lost. To be lost there has to be someplace else you're supposed to be, or would rather be, and in my case it was never true. I'd discovered that freedom is a journey without a destination and the very things I used to despise about public transport were the things I now loved; the arbtirary routes, clockwork regularity, the perfect anonymity of the transfer or coins, the inflexible demand for exact change.

Drivers and Transit Supervisors were my witless accomplices in complex escapes. I'd ride to the end of a line or get off at a random stop and walk, doubling back on foot, cutting through strange malls and neighbourhoods, crossing schoolyards and parking lots until I came to a stop on another line, another accidental step in the roundabout journey back to my room in the old hotel.

I was harder to follow than a spy. A secret agent has a purpose, a rendezvous, a clandestine meeting with a contact at a safe house, a motive that makes him or her predictable. Except for the main streets, where the village idiot lives on, leaning on a mailbox making rude suggestions to any stranger waiting for the light to cross the intersection, I had no contacts other than pre-school children and dogs.

Little boys would explain the system of tracks and mounds they were scratching out of dirt with toy trucks, miniature civilizations of mud and plastic. Little girls would tell me about the personal relationships of their dolls. Now and then, I'd pass a young mother and the kids would become shy, remembering they weren't supposed to talk to strangers. The mothers eyed me warily or smiled faintly if I didn't measure up to the current profile of a rapist or child-molester.

The dogs fell into two groups; apparent strays who followed me for a few blocks on the hope of a kind word or a scratched head then turned back at some invisible border, and the ones who tried to rip my fucking legs off on sight.

There was no safe house for me. Sometimes when I walked through residential neighbourhoods, I'd get the feeling nobody really lived there, that the houses were all empty or not houses at all but stage fronts held up by flimsy scaffolding. It was only toward evening that they came alive, lit from within by the range-hood lights, dining room chandeliers and the cold cathode glow of a million tv sets. Then, like a Peeping Tom, I'd catch a glimpse of the life within, a young couple with their arms around each other in the harsh overhead glare of a kitchen, children tranced before the flickering of cartoons, a man or woman standing at a window in silhouette staring out at the gathering darkness or at me in defiance or fear, I never knew which.

It was only when I was actually on the buses that I ever really met any other people. On every bus there are a couple of loons who sit driving the driver crazy when they're not talking to everyone else who gets on. Head-cases with their bus passes pinned to baseball hats, addresses sewn into linings of coats for identification when they get so lost or so annoying that someone calls the cops to take them back to their cages. Aging European Communists who revile the Russians, deplore the failure of the great human social experiment, but who still proudly call themselves Marxists as they breathe cheap Bulgarian wine at you through bad teeth. Old women who call everyone Dear and Love in loud querulous English accents and don't know what the world's coming to. Beery obstreperous afternoon drunks who do know what the world's coming to and can't wait to tell it.

I'd met them all, just like I'd waited in every Loop and depot in the city for the bus that would finally pull in, just as I lit my last butt of course, and take me away to a place somewhere beyond the end of the line. I was still waiting, but the buses were still running.

There was one bus I never rode, one line I never followed, one neighbourhood I never walked through, and that was the crescent street in Richmond where I'd lived with my wife and, briefly, our child. I don't know why. I wasn't afraid of being recognized, some awkward encounter with a former neighbour. After five years, I doubted any of our upwardly-mobile neighbours were still around. They'd all have moved to Kits, West Van or Shaughnessy by now on the windfall profits of selling their big houses to wealthy immigrant Chinese.

Our house was like all the others on the short curved street, an architect's doodle that looked like the top of a mineshaft and was designed to maximize the illusion of space with skylights and bay and bubble windows. The illusion worked until you put furniture in the rooms and people started tripping over it and bumping into each other. Though superficially more complex, all the houses in the development were mirror images of each other or variations on a theme, just like the older suburbs I grew up in and the new developments of Del Mar style monster homes with their vaulted entrances, mock pillars, "great rooms," their thin California pastel stucco turning green with wet rot at the corners after only a few years.

The Blue Parrot

Once I'd taken the bus up to my parents' old neighbourhood, high on the side of Grouse Mountain, in the older suburbs of the Fifties and Sixties. The houses were all big post-and-beam boxes, with five bedrooms and rec rooms and two and a half bathrooms, but the streets were empty and silent. When I was a boy, swarms of kids commandeered the streets with homemade skateboards, made from cheap lumber and rollerskate wheels nailed to the bottom, cheap steel wheels that squared off after a few runs, or soapbox racers with wheels cannibalized from wagons and baby-buggies and primitive handbrakes that always failed on the first descent of the heart-stopping hills. We played soccer, baseball, and hockey in those streets, broke the big picture windows of the houses with a hundred pucks and balls, chased and fought and the big houses threw back the soprano echo of our chorused shrieks and the voices of our parents bellowing at us from porches and sundecks to take turns, play fair, don't throw rocks and stop picking on the youngest.

But hardly anyone with children could afford to live there now that the price of real estate had gone up as fast as the children grew up, leaving the big houses tenanted by aging couples who found the big yards harder to maintain each year and talked constantly of selling and moving to apartments or townhouses nearer the shopping malls and doctors offices.

Our old house had been painted a shade of beige unknown in my parents' era and most of the big Douglas firs in the front had been cut down by the new owner to improve the overview of the city. There were no bikes or lacrosse sticks lying the driveway, no balls in the ditches, since the ditches had been replaced by storm drains and curbed cement sidewalks that nobody was walking on. No battered kites dangled from the powerlines. The lines had been buried and the power-poles replaced with curved metal lighting poles whose pools of clear light turned every street corner into an empty stage where nothing would ever happen. No half-rebuilt sportscars rusted in the yards or carports. Our old house didn't look like anybody's home and I never went back.

The only other place I never went was where I was going. Not that I'd never been there before. It was just another neighbourhood, a little older than most, in a part of South Burnaby where nothing much had ever happened. The rain stopped as I got off the bus, leaving the streets glistening as the sun tried to shoulder it's way through the clouds. The front door of the house was opened by my former mother-in-law as I was taking the steps like a man mounting the gallows.

"Elaine isn't here," she said, before she said hello. I guess she was trying to reassure me that there wasn't going to be a scene. She had always been kind, or at least polite to me, even after Elaine and I split. I don't think she approved of the way Elaine handled things for a minute, but family loyalty kept her from criticizing her daughter to me. She gave me a cup of coffee in the warm old-fashioned kitchen that had always smelled of baking and spices. The house was very quiet.

"Lisa?" I asked after half a cup.

"Upstairs," she said, "She knows you're here, but I didn't think it was right to make her come down before she was ready. She's feeling a bit shy."

I nodded. She wasn't the only one. We were all feeling a little shy. Elaine's mother and I asked each other how we were. We were both fine. I didn't ask about Elaine and she didn't rub it in. There was batter in a brownish Medicine Hat crockery bowl on the sideboard and a rack of cookies in the oven, so she had something to do without having to fuss and we didn't have to start in on the weather.

From where I sat, I could see part of the dining room. I found myself staring at the silver framed black and white photograph of Elaine's father that presided over family dinners from the china cabinet. He'd died a few years before I met Elaine, having survived the war in Europe, the trials of postwar immigration to Canada with no money, an unpopular accent and a meritorious war record whose only drawback was that he happened to have earned his medals and promotions while fighting for the losing side, spine-smashing jobs on the green-chains of various mills, the uphill battle for promotion, first through the unions, then through the shark-infested waters of middle management, until he finally became a senior executive for one of the huge lumber companies who hold the forests of British Columbia like medieval fiefs. Then his heart wore out. He survived everything but success.

"You remind me of my Dad." Elaine told me once, complicating a romantic interlude on the couch with an evidently unresolved Electra complex. Realizing I was supposed to be flattered, I got mad, thinking not just about her father but my own, who stayed a fireman for twenty years because there was never any money left over for anything else while raising four kids. He'd died young too, probably as a result, they said, of beatings, malnutrition, deliberate abuse and neglect while a guest of the Japanese Imperial Army three decades before. Sent to defend one of the indefensible outposts of the British Empire, when he was eighteen he was already behind barbed-wire, having killed men and watched thousands more killed. The only question I faced at eighteen was where to find the party on the weekend.

"Don't ever say that," I snapped at Elaine, spoiling the mood, "Your father and mine were cut from a whole different cloth. I can't think of a single person I know who could stand up for five minutes to the shit they lived with all their lives."

And it wasn't just the men. There was Elaine's own mother, for instance, who ought to be making the best of her widowhood, taking cruises, going on junkets to Reno or Palm Springs, dyeing her hair a different colour every week and tipping muscled beach boys to rub on her sunscreen, instead of raising a five year old handicapped girl single-handed, while the child's mother ran around with boys in sportscars like a nymphomaniac cheerleader and the father watched the world go by through a twenty-six ounce telescope.

"I'm sorry, " I said, hardly aware I'd opened my mouth, "I'm sorry we've made it...so hard for you..."

She knew exactly what I was trying to say, even if I didn't.

"I do what has to be done," she said without bitterness, as though that explained everything.

That pretty much covered the difference between her

generation and ours. We never really had to do anything we didn't want to. If we had, maybe more of us would have had the courage to do the things we said we wanted to do.

Suddenly, Lisa was there, camouflaged by the floral print of her grandmother's skirt, peeking out with huge brown eyes, like a fairy in a meadow. I'd seen her only twice in as many years and she'd grown from a baby into a slim, elfin thing, a magic child from under a fern.

I put my hands out slowly so I wouldn't startle her, my fingers struggling clumsily with the gestures I'd rehearsed so often, alone in my tall room with a drink on the night table. My mouth formed the words as silently as my fingers. I didn't even know if she could read lips.

Confused by my clumsiness, she looked up at her grandmother who said, "She doesn't have all her letters yet. At school they teach them a kind of shorthand first. It's quicker."

With a few brief signs, Elaine's mother translated for me while I thought of how many evenings she must have spent in night school classrooms, smelling of chalk and children, to learn them. My daughter turned to me. There was a graceful flurry of signals, too quick for me to follow, not that I could have understood. Then she was gone. I heard her footsteps on the stairs.

"Lisa?" I called pointlessly. Elaine's mother tried to smile at me.

"She said, 'I love you, Daddy'," she translated through a bright film of unshed tears.

I nodded and stood up. I couldn't have spoken even if I'd had anything to say.

She seemed to be struggling for words herself, now that we had to use our voices alone.

"I think you should go now," she told me, "I don't think she'll come down again. I'm not sure these visits are a good idea...I don't mean to be cruel, but they're too...few and far between...I know it's hard for you, but it's so much harder for her...She gets so excited and upset, then she can't...well...."

The Blue Parrot

That's what real pain is; sharper than a long splinter driven into the quick under a fingernail, lonelier than a toothache in the middle of the night, more sickening than a hard kick in the balls — it's hearing your own neccessary fictions, your own most precious lies and rationalizations parrotted back to you as the truth.

"I know," I stammered, stumbling to the door.

As I took the steps two at a time, a bright red Porsche pulled up in front. The sun had come out and the top was down. Elaine was sitting in the passenger seat beside a young guy who looked like every bit of character he possessed was in his moustache. She had on one of those snotty looks she always wore so well until she saw my face. Then it changed to something terribly wounded, almost loving, but I was already gone, striding down the block. I was in no mood for the farcical amenities of introduction to the new model boyfriend.

When I hit the main drag, I jumped the first bus I saw without clocking its destination or direction. After a few blocks, I bailed. I knew I'd never make it to the end of the line. I was gone as soon as a spotted one of those slick motor hotels licensed for a pub and lounge. A lost traveller in the asphalt desert, I needed an oasis of plastic palms where all the sand was in the lobby's standing ashtrays and everything beyond the smoked glass windows was only a mirage.

Chapter 11

Looking back, I guess I should have seen it coming. Maybe, with some kind of psychic peripheral vision, I did, because what happened next surprised me less than it might have done. It had been over a week since I'd seen Lisa in the bar and I knew Pat must be back or she'd have been in touch. When they finally turned up at The Blue Parrot, I knew from the way they came in together, from the way he guided her to the bar she'd have had to have total amnesia to forget, Something Had Happened.

Fishermen have a careful catty walk , knowing one sloppy step on a slippery pitching deck can be the last, but I sensed a modest strut in Pat's stride. From the way she let him order her glass of white wine, looked at him, leaned against his shoulder unselfconsciously at the bar, I gathered it was mutual, whatever it was.

I gave her credit for one thing right then. She didn't fuss over him, play with his hair or his tie, talk baby-talk or shriek at his jokes that way some women do in that situation, like she-wolves making something out of playing with the lead male to let the other girls know where they stand in the pack. They were still easy together. They were just different. They weren't just together, they were Together.

I bought them the first round that night and they understood without asking. I bought myself one and we drank to each other, grinning like idiot conspirators whose homemade bomb has actually gone off on time. At least I knew what I was grinning about.

I'd been having a hard time, especially after closing, forgetting that moment in the dark with Lisa before the cat fight when we had wanted each other as dumbly and blindly as two human beings can. The look she'd given me that night I got drunk in the bar still haunted the eighty-proof hallucinations that passed for my dreams.

I just couldn't see the sense in it. I knew I'd feel uneasy around Pat if I sent her home to his place after being with me in my room and even uneasier under his roof. I couldn't see Lisa and I furtively groping and slobbering on one another every time he was out of the room, like guilty teenagers, or carrying on some kind of secret affair while he was out on the boat.

It was all too silly, but it was seriously silly because they were my friends and, all things considered, I was almost happy for the first time in a long time. I didn't want things to change between us. Nobody's ever content to leave well enough alone. Maybe it's because well enough never seems like it when more always seems to be just within reach. I'd already wised up to the fact that you always get more than you bargained for with somebody else. Nobody just is who they are. They're the sum of their past and you inherit it all, the failures, traumas, neuroses, relatives, friends, enemies, obsessions, irritating habits, the works.

There is a Point of No Return in life. It doesn't have a rest stop parking lot or picnic tables to encourage you to pull over and get your bearings or take in the view, so most of us drive on by without recognizing it. But once you've passed it, there's no going back, no starting fresh from scratch or with a clean slate, no new beginnings. All you can do is put the hammer down and press on with an out of date map on the console, one eye on the gas gauge and one eye on the road.

So when Pat and Lisa came in that night and I saw how it was with them, I was relieved, the way you are when you're confronted with a difficult decision you suddenly don't have to make. They didn't stay long and it got to be a rare shaker of a night, so there was no opportunity for awkward silences or forced conversation. I was too busy pouring to check my emotional underwear for tell-tale ambivalent stains.

Marion and Helen, the part-time waitress, were calling out orders like floor traders on the Commodities Exchange and I was holding my own with both hands. Tending bar is a simple job. Any of the higher primates can be taught to do it in about an hour, but like everything else, there's a difference between doing it and doing it well.

When you're doing it right, you whip bottles up out of the wells with two fingers, putting just enough english on the wrist so they hang suspended at chest height for a second. You catch them on the fly and free-pour straight from the shoulder, shooting a perfect one-and-a-quarter stream of liquor through the smoking air and into the glass your left hand has just swept through the ice and lifted to catch the shot. Do the last part wrong and you can break a glass in your ice sink, which is why you always have two, plus a backup bucket, because otherwise everything comes to a screaming halt, especially the Manager.

When you're on, all the shouted conversations in the room blend with the music into one continuous roar, but you can hear a cocktail waitress order from fifty feet away. Bottles and glasses leap into your hands, which seem to have grown larger, webbed and slightly sticky, imbued with amphibian grace and sureness. Everything happens as if at the command of a methaphetamined Sorcerer's Apprentice, which is what you look like, surrounded by shimmering phials of exotic essences, emerald Creme de Menthe, cobalt Blue Curacao, carmine Campari, canary Advocaat, liquors and liqueurs in a hundred delicate shades of amber and gold, each uniquely shaped bottle containing it's own particular genie or demon.

When it was over, I felt loose and good. I'd been sipping the last hour or so, not enough to make me sloppy, but just to take the edge off the adrenaline. I'd been back-chatting the girls all night like a pep-talking first base coach, telling them how hot they were, that with two girls like them I could win the Nobel Prize for Mixology, get myself called to the bar, across the bar and behind bars.

The Blue Parrot

I let Helen go a little before closing to save her a few bucks on the baby-sitter and get her out of my hair. She was twenty-seven and just out-growing the fluffy blonde cuteness that had defined her for ten years. According to Marion, she also had a mild crush on me, but she had two little girls and a husband who was always leaving her and coming back when he was broke and I didn't need that kind of trouble.

I'd almost forgotten about Pat and Lisa and I didn't think Marion had even noticed the subtle change in their relationship, but I underestimated her intuition, as usual. The last of the Last Call Cowboys had been rounded up and out, grumbling and sucking their ice cubes. We were alone in the bar, she was bent over cashing out her float and I made some crack about it having been more interesting than a weekend in a Norwegian baseball training-camp. Then I noticed the tears carving twin canyons through the strata of her makeup. I didn't know what to do, so I did what I do. I poured her a stiff one. She downed it at a gulp, but it didn't help. It seemed to set her off.

"Men are such fools!" she sobbed, "She'll destroy him."

I thought this was a bit over the top, but I didn't get much time to think about it because she threw herself at me and started soaking my shoulder like an East End Italian watering the tomato bed. I patted her back and held her, all the things friends are required to do at times like that. Then, for the second time in too short a while, I was being kissed in a fashion far from friendly.

"Take me upstairs," Marion whispered.

Marion was a mechanic's calendar fantasy in the flesh, but I was tired, wound up, half-shot and the manufacturer's guarantee on the reinforced crotch of my slacks wasn't getting any kind of stress test from me.

"Look....Marion..." I started to mumble.

"Take me upstairs," she demanded desperately.

I had nothing to argue with. Grabbing a bottle of vodka from the bar, I led her, with stops for longer and saltier kisses, up the narrow stairs to my tall, dark strange room. She wouldn't let me put on a light, not even the bedside gooseneck lamp. I went through the motions of hospitality like a blind butler, groping for glasses I hoped were clean to get us a drink, but she caught me and pulled me back against those hard-wired breasts and tightly sheathed hips.

"Marion?...For Chrissakes..."

She muzzled me with her lips. I knew she was only trying to use me to get even somehow, but she couldn't have picked a less appropriate tool, so to speak.

When she broke away, I sighed with relief for the second time that night, thinking we could have a snort, talk about things and break it up gently. Seconds later, I heard the soft unmistakeable whizz of zippers and whisper of nylon and lycra peeling away from flesh. The bed creaked ominously. Feeling like a fool, I dropped my laundry and kneeled on the bed, feeling around for her hand to establish a sane point of contact in the dark. She found me first and pulled me down against her feverish length, thrusting her tongue so deep in my mouth she could have done a tonsillectomy in passing.

I ran my hand cursorily over her loosened breasts. It seemed like the polite thing to do under the circumstances and it was by no means unpleasant work. She was silky and yielding everywhere, the way men like a woman in the dark, even if they do stare at the hard young bodies on the beach. But it simply wasn't happening. I was blind from the waist down.

With a groan, she began to administer the kind of oral first aid women resort to in such emergencies, but I grabbed her shoulders and held her still.

"Marion?...Please...don't..."

She rolled away, crying quietly.

"It's not your fault..." I started to say, feeling her immediately stiffen beside me. It was the wrong thing to say. That's what you say to somebody when you really mean you think it is their fault and you want them to feel guilty without a fight.

We lay together, each alone in our separate Hells, for a long time. Finally, I lit a cigarette. It was still dark enough that I didn't need the blindfold.

The Blue Parrot

"Well, she's got you both. She's got you too..." Marion said softly, when she got her voice back under control, "That witch has put her spell on you both. It's not fair..."

She didn't say anything more, just got up, gathered her clothes and found the bathroom. Women have toilet radar, they can always find the bathroom in any strange dark place. She turned on the overhead light in the little room as she was shutting the door and I caught a glimpse of spindly legs, drooping buttocks, creased belly and flaccid breasts, the beehive hairdo frayed in all directions like the mane of a demented crone from a fairy tale. In that instant of cruelly harsh unshaded hundred watt light, I saw the old woman she was becoming.

I managed to get my underwear on backwards and a t-shirt inside out by the time she came out. There was a faint grey light in the room that made her look very old, in spite of the amazing repairs she'd accomplished in the bathroom. She didn't want a drink or a cigarette and she didn't want to talk, which was a relief. In a murmur, she told me not to bother coming down to the lobby. She'd call a cab on the direct line from there.

At the door, she said sadly, "I feel sorry for you. I pity you both." Then she was gone, carrying her stiletto heels. She didn't make a sound on the stairs.

I found a few half-melted ice cubes in the cooler under the bed and built myself a very strong drink, thinking about what she said, about Lisa having put her spell on Pat and I. I could understand how she'd see it that way. I could even understand how it might seem fitting that she and I should get each other, at least for one night, as a kind of consolation prize. Except that there isn't much real consolation in revenge. It's like the Bloody Mary you drink to kill your hangover. You can dress it up with Tabasco and Lea & Perrins and slices of lime or cucumber, sticks of munchable celery, but it's still just the early hours of another brutal morning after.

Sitting at the tall window, sipping my lukewarm nightcap, I could just make out the driver slumped behind the wheel of a cab parked on the stand east of Lonsdale. A minute later, he sat up, started his engine and idled along the block to stop beneath my window. I heard the staccatto rap of Marion's heels on the sidewalk, but I didn't look over to watch. High over the city, the clouds flushed pink as a whore's bathroom as the sun began to shoulder it's way through the crowd of mountains behind me. The cab's door slammed with a dull metallic thud and the car purred away down the empty silent street.

Chapter 12

I was glad the next day was Sunday, because I wouldn't have to face Marion until Monday night. When I came to, a bit before noon, I poured the rest of the bottle of vodka into a large Thermos with a lot of cold water and hopped a bus west to Ambleside Beach. It was hot and crowded. An assortment of young steaks and steakettes were basting and barbecuing themselves on the sandy altar of summer and it was pleasant to be among them, surrounded by the heavy sensual scent of their broiling bodies. I felt like a monk at an orgy. I rated a giggling glance or two, just to remind me I was human, but I wasn't trying it on. With my dark glasses, my upside down book and my trusty canteen, I was Mister X.

Sunday is a good day to do nothing because you don't have to feel guilty about it. Not everybody looks at it that way. Stores, malls and bars are all open Sundays now, all implying that there's something you ought to be doing, even if it's only buying more shit you don't want or making up for missing the party the night before by sitting in a beer-parlour playing bingo for cuts of beef.

Some people devote Sundays to hobbies. They restore vintage cars, build unneccesary additions onto their houses, do cabinet work, arrange stamps from dirty and exotic countries in immaculate albums, refinish dubious antiques scavenged at flea-markets or paint landscapes and seascapes that wind up over the mantle in the living room, a challenge to the critical vocabularies and tact of their guests.

Before my daughter was born and I discovered the full possiblilites of vodka, I had a hobby myself. Mine was Lepidoptera. It only sounds like something that could get you a course of shots from the doc or ten years in the crowbar hotel. I used to collect butterflies. Every spring and summer weekend, while other men were playing with their power tools or weeding and feeding their lawns, I'd drive out to the Fraser Valley and wander the hills and fields with my fine mesh net and my killing jar.

I wasn't wanton about it. Like any good hunter, I was only interested in really superb trophy specimens, which are few and a long time between. More often than not, I was content to come home after a long day rambling in the open with nothing in the jar. When I did spot a pair of wings worthy of my mesh, I had the thrill of the chase and stalk, the rapture of the capture and the kill was as humane as possible.

The killing jar was fitted with a small filter capsule in the lid, into which a few drops of a chloroform derivative were poured to put the butterfly to sleep before it died. Its purpose was to prevent the victim from damaging itself in panic as it suffocated, but it made for a gentle, at times even beautiful ceremony of death. At home, I applied another fluid, called Relaxing Fluid, which stopped the insects from becoming too brittle to handle for mounting. I carried my own personal supply of relaxing fluid in a leather bound silver flask my wife had given me for a birthday present in an attempt at barbed wit.

I couldn't blame her for resenting my hobby. After all, her friends and neighbours husbands, brandishing their pistol-grip Black and Deckers, produced pannelled rec rooms, extended kitchens with skylights and freestanding islands surfaced in butcher's block, swing sets, jungle-gyms, coffee tables cut from immense burls and sheathed in numberless coats of dustless clear plastic laquer. All I produced were tastefully mounted and framed butterflies which, according to her, made our guests itchy all over. I could have understood that if my hobby had been collecting spiders.

"But, they're beautiful," I protested, "And they're not bugs. They're butterflies."

The Blue Parrot

"They're bugs and they're creepy," she insisted. "It's sick."

She took to referring to my hobby as "buggery", a play on words she found hilarious and repeated, with variations, at every opportunity.

"Going buggering again, honey?" she would shriek sarcastically from behind the lawnmower as I left on one of my rambles. Every head on the block would snap up from it's marigold borders and BMW cut-waxing. God and everybody else on the block knew what the neighbours thought.

I did try to initiate her into the mysteries, to arouse some spasm of admiration for Rhopalocera, the Nymphalidae, the Papilionadae, the Hesperidiiae. I saw us traversing the fluttering fields together, a picnic basket and His and Hers nets in hand, falling into some fragrant furrow while majestic Monarchs flitted above our fused forms and a magnificent winged thing elegantly expired in the killing jar.

It was no use. The bugs and the bugger were banished to the Den, that temporary place of exile for husbands which is soon rechristened The Nursery and redecorated. Then all the impedimentia of his final boyish enthusiasms, the models of formula race cars, football trophies and team pictures, ships in bottles and unfinished novels, are relegated to the attic to moulder until the inevitable spring cleaning when they'll be put out with the trash or hauled to the dump.

The municipal dump, now called the "landfill site" or, even more sensitively, the "recycling centre," is the saddest place in the civilized world. It's always located in a swampy or wooded area. As you approach it, the houses thin out and get a depressed, derelict look. Few realtors host open houses in these neighbourhoods. There is a shack at the gate and you have to stop and answer to the bloated grimy Rhadamanthus stationed there. You may be required to provide a pedigree of residence for his ponderous inspection. Municipalities are fussy about their rubbish. They don't want any foreign trash cluttering up their dump.

Once admitted, you drive up a dusty gravel track through

great earth barrows, huge tumuli raised by bulldozers which are forever burying the waste of gracious living in a vast midden. At last, you come to the Golgotha of garbage, where you try to back up as close as possible to the most recent pile of refuse without getting stuck in it. As soon as you get out of the car, you want a bath.

It is always a warm overcast day. There are clouds of fat buzzing flies, drunk on fermenting filth. Fires smoulder as garbage is burned before being buried. Greasy cinders float on the hot stinking wind, burning your cheeks. A few gutted cars are the only landmarks. Before you stretches a vista of every object made by the hand of man — broken, smashed, stained, crumpled, ripped, torn, vomited and excreted upon, terminally exhausted and abandoned.

Beyond, where the dozers are hardest at work, is the great pit into which the municipal garbage trucks disgorge their never-ending loads, like mechanical bowel movements. Wheeling above, endlessly rising and descending, flocks of black and white birds, crows and gulls, images of antithesis dispute the choicest bits of shit.

You unload as quick as you can, flinging your trash over your shoulder, harassed by wasps, and get the Hell out of there. You don't roll down the windows until you're blocks away. When you get home, you do take a bath.

One day, when I'd been nagged out of a butterfly expedition and into a trip to the dump, with the back of the Volvo station wagon loaded with the debris which accumulates even in the most fastidious households, I found myself dawdling to watch the man parked next to me. He was about fifty, thick through the middle and almost bald, but well dressed in the kind of golf shirt and slacks combination that manages to casually look expensive. He was leaning against the back fender of a big sedan, a new Buick or Chrysler, something long and wide and comfortable, and he was looking mournfully into the trunk.

He seemed to be taking his time about his business, which was unusual, since he looked like the dynamic executive type. Ignoring the pestering wasps, he would take out an old book with the covers torn off, leaf through it, then tentatively put it back in the trunk. Then he would pick out a sports trophy with one arm snapped off the gilt figure, sag meditatively against the car and reluctantly consign it to the edge of the pile, as though he didn't want to lose sight of it or have it get too dirty, in case he changed his mind.

On a busy weekend at the dump, you can't help noticing other people's garbage any more than you can avoid seeing someone else's underwear at the laundromat. Still, it's not polite to stare. If the plain, myopic skinny girl at the coin laundry drops an armload of black lacy bras, garter-belts and multi-coloured panties that wouldn't decently cover a vaccination scar, you pick them up, reload her basket, say "You're welcome" to her "Thank you" and don't even blink, let alone wink. Her lingerie is none of your business. This guy's trash was none of my mine. The things he was throwing away didn't seem remarkable. They looked like the typical traces of boyhood; faded pennants and wingless model airplanes, an old tube radio, a pair of horse-head bookends, the ears cropped unevenly from being knocked off desks — odds and ends that wouldn't fetch fifty cents at a garage sale.

It wasn't until I heard him sigh, almost groan, that I realized he was weeping. His chubby well-shaved cheeks glistened in the harsh flat light. Maybe he was remembering a friend, a son estranged or dead, or maybe just his own lost youth. I don't know and it doesn't really matter, but for a moment, as I looked at the bits and pieces he'd placed on the dump, they took on the eerie poignance of the burial goods of a young Pharaoh, the model barges, the child-size chariot and bow, the sad regalia of the tomb.

The back of my Volvo station wagon was full of boxes, neatly taped shut by my wife. I had no idea what was in any of them. A lot of strange things turn up in the dump; winning lottery tickets, bundles of cash, body parts in plastic bags, foetuses in jars. I unloaded the boxes without opening them as fast as I could and got the hell out of there.

I suppose my butterfly collection wound up on a dump somewhere. I didn't take anything with me when I left and I'd actually given up collecting long before that. It happened one night when I was mounting a fine large specimen I'd netted that afternoon. I'd removed it from the killing jar and fixed it to a soft board on the desk with a long pin while I prepared it's framed sarcophagus. My wife pounded on the door of the den.

"What are you doing in there?" she whined.

"Mounting," I snapped.

"I should be so lucky," she quipped, as she stomped off to bed.

When I looked around, the butterfly's wings were slowly moving up and down. I'd been a little short on chloroform, but it had been motionless in the killing jar for hours. As I watched, fascinated, it pulled itself free of the board and, still impaled by the pin, began dragging itself sluggishly toward the edge of the desk and the open window beyond.

I reached out and pinched it lightly by one trembling wing. Removing the pin as gently as possible, I cupped the butterfly in my hand and lowered it out the window into the shrubbery below. It wasn't there in the morning. Maybe a bird got it, or maybe it escaped, revived by the fresh air, at first light. Butterflies don't live long anyway. But it had risen from the dead and that was enough for me. I took my collection down off the walls that night and put it, my net and the killing jar in the attic. My wife said nothing, but simply looked smug, imagining she'd got her own way again.

I never told her the real reason and I never went out into the hills and fields again. Now and then I go to the beach and watch young things in brightly coloured bathing suits flit and flutter across the hot sand.

As it turned out, I needn't have worried so much about Marion. When we finally had to face each other across the bar the next day, she was subdued, a bit distant, but friendly enough to commiserate over the weapons-grade plutonium sunburn I picked up from drinking and snoozing at the beach.

Chapter 13

I didn't see Pat and Lisa for a couple of weeks. It didn't bother me. I assumed they were doing what most couples do when they discover that wonderful thing they can do which always bears repeating. One morning, when I'd been woken up early by a City crew making unusually enthusiastic repairs to the undulating pavement in front of the hotel, I decided to drop in on the happy couple, more out of boredom than anything else.

I found them hard at work. It seemed to be that kind of morning. Lisa answered the door in coveralls, her bandanaed hair sprinkled with wood shavings and dots of paint. She was disappointed and delighted to see me.

"I wanted it to be a surprise," she gushed, "But now I'm so glad you're here."

She led me through the house. I didn't see Pat but I heard sawing noises from the basement workshop. They had knocked out the back wall of the living room and enclosed part of the sundeck beyond it with a half-wall topped by glass to form a bright, airy weathertight arcade, like a sunroom, except that it was properly roofed over.

"Isn't it wonderful?" Lisa demanded.

"It might be, if I knew what it was," I said.

"It's an aviary, silly."

"An aviary?"

"A birdhouse. Isn't it wonderful?" she repeated with unquenchable joy.

I nodded cautiously. "It certainly is big. Just what kind of bird are you planning on getting? A Bald Eagle? Andean Condor?" Poor Felix, I thought. He'd be like a starving man confronting a frisky bull. All that beef and no way to get it onto the barbecue.

"Birds," she replied, pluralizing the notion for me. "Parrots. Big parrots...then, when nature takes it's course, little parrots."

"Parrots?" I must've sounded dubious, thick or both.

The idea was, she explained, they were going to breed and raise parrots and sell them, privately and to pet shops. Her pogey had run out and she hadn't been able to find a job. Pat was being just wonderful about it, she told me. In fact, he'd encouraged her to stay at home, but she needed to feel she was making a contribution. This way, she'd still be around the house, but she'd be taking care of the birds and making money, too.

The plan wasn't as crazy as it sounded. Parrots are very expensive birds. I knew they could cost up to a grand, retail. I also knew that they're hard to import because they can carry Newcastle Disease, which is fatal to domestic chickens and turkeys, as well as a fever from their native Central American jungles which they can transmit to human beings. I'd read something about Parrot Fever somewhere, enough to know it could kill you. So it made sense to raise them locally. Sort of.

I wasn't about to knock the idea, anyway, since she was so obviously sold on it, giving me the grand tour of the nearly finished aviary, pointing out the extra insulation and double-glazed windows to keep the birds warm year round. She even told me she got the idea about the parrots from me. I knew this was just flattery to include me in, but the image of the parrot, outlined in pale blue neon in the window of the bar where she met Pat through me, may have been printed on the back of her mind, like a double-exposed flim.

Downstairs, I had a short snort with Pat in his workshop. Short because it was before noon and while he could be a hard-drinking fisherman, he was also too methodical a man to drink around power tools. He was constructing perches out of various gauges of dowelling, drilling neat sockets into the thicker uprights and tapping in the narrower perches, each with a neat dab of creamy wood glue on the end going into the hole. The whole idea might be bird-brained, but I could see those perches were going to be marvellous, perfectly fitted, horizontal, yet part of a harmonious assymetrical design he had sketched on the back of an old phone bill with the stub of a thick, flat carpenter's pencil.

I made polite noises about the aviary and the perches while he worked, without commenting on the overall wisdom of the project, which I thought was cleverly tactful, until Pat tipped me just a hint of a wink with the corner of an eye. I realized he thought the idea was as crazy as a honeymoon at the North Pole too, but neither of us said anything about it.

I tried not to add up what it all must be costing him. Mind you, Pat knew a lot of people, never paid the retail rate for anything but drinks, always swung a deal, which at the current price of salmon wasn't hard, and did all his own work. He was enoying himself, indulging Lisa. Making her happy was making him happy and he could afford the tariff.

Being around all that activity was making me feel conspicuously idle, so I left before either of them could think of something for me to do and set off in search of an ambiance less at variance with my inclinations.

I was invited back to celebrate the arrival of the first male and female breeding pair and, after that, new ones seemed to have materialized every time I dropped in. In no time there were at least a dozen birds in the aviary. I lost count and would have lost interest but for Lisa's unflagging enthusiasm. She cleaned the aviary daily, scraping up the guano to be dumped in the flower garden as fertilizer for now, though she talked of selling that, too. She mopped the floor, fed and watered the big birds, wandering among them cooing and talking, calm and unconcerned. I knew enough about parrots to know you couldn't get me in there on a bet. They could take off a man's finger with one snip of that powerful undercurved beak. They never bothered Lisa though. She had a way with them, just like she did with Felix.

She became a self-taught authority on parrots and I learned more about them than I ever wanted to know. I imagine Pat bore the brunt of this ornithological outpouring, but he never showed any sign of boredom or impatience as she prattled on about the evolution and history of the parrot, the care and feeding of parrots, the vocabulary potential of parrots, the mating habits of parrots and so on.

On the last score, she couldn't communicate her enthusiasm to the birds. Aside from the occasional raucous squabble over perch-protocol, they remained as superficially disinterested in each other as teenagers at a high school dance. Lisa was undaunted.

"They're just getting settled," she said in an authoritative tone.

Originally, she hadn't planned to teach them to talk, leaving that to the discretion of their future owners, but I guess she couldn't resist trying to teach them a few words. Every time she entered the aviary, she was greeted with a chorus of raspy voices repeating, "I love you, Lisa. I love you, Lisa. I love you, Lisa."

The only one more interested in the birds than Lisa was, of course, Felix. He patrolled the perimeter of the aviary constantly, from the living room to the sundeck, peering in at the birds with obvious intent. It was just as well for him he couldn't get at them. Any one of them would have made parrot-bait out of him in an instant.

I think what hit Felix hardest wasn't Lisa's neglect of him, because she still waited on him hand and foot, but the parrots' total indifference to his pantherish posings at their windows. As if their collective genetic memory reminded them that jaguars were much bigger than Felix, they remained unflappable as he postured around them like the great jungle cat he probably thought he was after a few drinks.

As the summer wore out, I spent less time up at Pat's. They didn't come into The Blue Parrot as often, either. Lisa and Marion were scrupulously and frostily polite to one another when they did. Lisa seemed to sense she'd stepped in something there. I couldn't see

The Blue Parrot

Pat telling her anything about Marion, even if there was anything to tell. He wasn't the type to worry over nuances of emotional tone and I certainly never said anything.

Part of the reason I didn't go to Pat's as often was the aviary. We tended to sit there, drinking and watching the aviary where the view had been, like it was an enormous tv set showing a documentary on parrots with Lisa doing the voice-over narration and Felix lurking around the edge of the screen. After a few such evenings, it got to be like watching PBS National Geographic re-runs or a video of somebody's Mexican vacation you've already seen.

I couldn't figure out how Pat stood it, until I realized he was truly in love with Lisa. I knew he was fond of her, enjoyed having a woman around the house again and was doubtlessly experiencing that renewal of horizontal vigour a young woman can provoke in an older man. I'd noticed he was taking better care of himself, shedding a few pounds around the middle and dressing only a decade out of fashion rather than the usual quarter-century, but I put that down to the understandable vanity of a man who knows he's lucky. Of course, I knew that that the trouble with getting a new lease on life is that the rent always goes up at the same time and it's usually more than you can afford to pay. Pat just seemed too real, too sensible to do anything as flaky as falling in love. After all, it was the kind of thing I might have done, but for a cat fight on a hot summer night.

I only discovered Pat was deeply and truly in love with Lisa one afternoon when he came into The Blue Parrot alone for a cool one on his way home. It had been hot enough to blister paint all day and he'd been down at the marina in the worst of it, working on the boat. He told me he'd painted a new name on her stern. I didn't need three guesses.

"It's important to have the right name on the stern of your boat," he informed me seriously.

Routinely, I asked why, but I almost wished I hadn't.

"Well, if you're a fisherman who works alone, like I do, and something happens, you go over the side, probably the last thing you're ever going to see is the stern of your own boat going away."

Even in the heat, I felt a chill when he said that. It was probably just the air-conditioning in the bar, working for a change.

After he left, I thought about the superstitions of sailors, that it was bad luck to change the name of a ship, bad luck to have a woman on board because the ship, always called "she", might somehow be jealous. Things that sound like a lot of bilgewater, but The Blue Parrot was a waterfront bar and I had seen the palms of sailors, like Old Al's, tattooed with a single blue star, a Celtic charm against drowning that was ancient when Jesus Christ was only a gleam in the Holy Ghost's omniscient eye.

For Pat to rename his boat after Lisa was like turning broadside in a running gale. He could only be in love and it would be that final, terrible love that comes just when you think it will never come again, like a voice that whispers of freedom just when you have accepted your life sentence in the solitary confinement of the heart.

Chapter 14

Opinions are supposed to be like assholes; everybody's got one but it's not polite to talk about it in public. That doesn't seem to stop anybody from telling you about their opinions, on any subject, at any time of the day or night, whether you're interested or not. On the whole, I'm not sure it wouldn't be an improvement if they talk about the other, just for a change.

Of course, it's always their "honest opinion". That's what justifies them telling you something they know you don't want to hear, something that will embarrass you, hurt your feelings, maybe plunge you into suicidal despair or murderous rage. But it's okay, because they're being honest. They can sleep the sleep of the just while you're tap-dancing in the air at the end of a rope over the rafter or shooting down strangers with a 30.30 from a tenth-floor window. There's always a lot of bogus bottled sincerity debasing the currency of conversation and, more often than not, honesty is just the apron of virtue cruelty puts on when it's got a particularly bloody hatchet job in hand.

Everybody had an opinion about Pat and Lisa, as soon as they found out how it was, and I wasn't interested in any of them, especially over breakfast in the Sunrise Cafe. I was losing a staring contest with my two fried eggs when Geoff the barber slipped into the Mac-Tac panelled booth across from me. The styrofoam coffee cup in his hand exuded a strong smell of rye. He tipped a generous share into my thick stoneware mug and waited while I downed it. I must've looked like I was feeling better. Appearances can be deceiving.

"Say, you know this girl who's living with Pat pretty well, don't you?" he asked.

"She hasn't killed any of my near relatives and she doesn't owe me money," I said. I hoped he'd let it go at that, but nobody ever does.

"You know what I mean," he said impatiently, "I mean, what kind of person is she?"

I shrugged. "I know her well enough to know she buys her own drinks most of the time, takes in stray cats and she's a fair cook," I admitted.

"She's a bit of a stray herself, though, isn't she? I mean, the way I heard it, you introduced her to Pat when..."

"And what they do on their own time is their business," I finished for him. I leaned hard on the pronouns, hoping he'd get the message.

"I know. I know. It's just that everybody's talking and nobody seems to know anything..."

I shouldn't have put him on the spot, especially after the way I'd pumped him for the goods on Pat when I wanted to cover my own ass. He and Pat and Marion were part of an older community, disappearing behind the fake distressed-brick facades of waterfront condo projects and gifts shops that sold forty buck t-shirts with authentic Native designs. Lisa and I were newcomers, pikers in their world, and I should have felt for him. After all, bartenders and barbers and cabdrivers all have to put up with the same marathon song and dance of sports, politics, money and sex, death and taxes and gossip from a clientele who expects them to know everything from last night's hockey score and this morning's Bank of Canada prime rate to who won the fifth race at Exhibition Park this afternoon and what colour panties the coffee-shop waitress is wearing today.

If I'd known this back when I was in advertising, I could've saved the agency a fortune in polls, telemarket surveys and database management. All you have to do is get a haircut, take a cab to the nearest bar and, by the time you're on your second drink, you'll have all the "public opinion" you can keep down.

Still, the situation had changed. Pat and Lisa were my friends and I wasn't about to return favour for favour on a professional basis with Geoff at their expense. If Geoff was getting a hard time for not being able to dish up the hottest gossip, it was his tough luck. But he looked like more than that was bothering him.

"Look," he said, "I'm only asking because Pat came in for a haircut yesterday and things got, well, a little out of hand..."

"Out of hand?" I said, "Geoff, if you're leading up to something, take the shortcut 'cause you've lost me already."

He sighed heavily, and a wave of whisky fumes made me light-headed.

"Like I said, Pat came in for a haircut yesterday and he took the other chair 'cause I had a customer. This girl, Lisa whatever, was sitting on the bus bench out front, getting a suntan while she waited for Pat, I guess, wearing one of those boob-tube halter things and playing with a cat..."

"I know the cat," I interjected. He gave me a look like I was missing the point.

"Anyways," he went on, "I finished and Pat was still in the chair and this young buck came in and sat in mine. Now, he took a good look at the girl on the way in, but that's not a hanging offense and she's worth looking at. I don't know whether he'd had a couple of beers at the Olympic or the Parrot or what it was, but he had kind of a smart mouth..."

"Uh-huh," I said non-committally, getting a creepy feeling that put me even further off my eggs .

"Well, you know," Geoff said uncomfortably, "He started talking too loud...Saying things like 'Hey baby, I'd sure like to play with your pussy'...That kind of thing..."

"A regular Oscar Wilde," I observed.

"Who?" Geoff said.

"Never mind. You don't cut his hair and I don't pour his drinks. What happened?"

"Anyway, the next thing I know," Geoff said, "Pat steps out of his chair in the middle of his haircut, pulls the sheet off, grabs this punk's arm with one hand and bends it back over the armrest like he's gonna snap it at the elbow. It all happened so fast that old Stan, the part-timer whose been cutting Pat's hair is still snipping away at nothing...The kid starts to mouth Pat off, but Pat pinched his windpipe with his free hand. Then he started in on me, for Chrissakes! Not even looking at the kid, who's turning blue at the gills, telling me he's had his last haircut in my place until I clean out the goddamn riff-raff! Me, who's been cutting his hair since he could walk and old enough to be his father..."

He was genuinely bewildered. "Jesus," he said, "There hasn't been a scrap in that barbershop since the nineteen-fifty-seven Grey Cup and I won that one, so I thought I'd better quit while I was ahead. But this, Christ, I've never seen Pat so hot and wild in all the years I've known him. I thought he was going to cripple that kid for life and take a round out of me just for being there....I mean, he must love that girl something terrible."

"Yeah," I said, "I guess you could put it like that."

"God help him," Geoff said, "That's why I asked you what kind of person she is. I mean, a guy his age...a girl like that..."

"Like what, Geoff?" I said grumpily, "They're just two people trying to hold each other's heads above water and salvage what they can from the shipwreck of life. They might even have half a chance, if everybody would just leave them alone to make the best of it....As for that shit-pants clown in the barbershop, if it had been your wife or girlfriend or daughter or any woman you know he was mouthing off about, you'd have slapped your straight-razor up against his Adam's apple and offered to shave him down to the shoulders if he didn't watch his lip."

There was a trio of voices from the next booth.

"And a good thing too..."

"I should hope so..."

"Disgraceful behaviour..."

It was The Aunts in the booth behind, the Weird Sisters,

having tea and scones and eavesdropping as shamelessly as only old ladies can. A chorus of fuddled Furies. Fates with the Dts.

"Such a sweet girl..."

"Such a nice man..."

"So happy together..."

"A girl needs an older man. My dear departed was twelve years older than ..."

"A man needs a young woman. Why, I was only sixteen when..."

"Youth and wisdom..."

"A man is still...a man..."

"And so much in love..."

Like I said, everyone has an opinion.

"Biddies," Old Al growled, sliding into the booth on my side, "Dry holes. What do they know?"

I'd noticed him hobbling in to perch on the fountain stool nearest the booth, like a buzzard taking a low perch near something about to die, which, under the circumstances, I assumed was me. I could've asked him the same question. What did he know but the whores of half a dozen continents and the three or four women who'd got him drunk enough to marry them in forgotten ports of call. He had children, probably grand-children, he'd never seen, probably didn't know existed. He was the paterfamilias of a further flung clan than any diaspora could have sown and what he knew about domesticity, the comforts of hearth and home, amounted to some port of registry, a legal convenience, the name of an alien city in painted letters fading on a rusty stern.

"Women want three things," he pronounced, "Money and children, both if they can get them, and a safe harbour most of all."

My breakfast had turned into an inedible greasy centrepiece. I nodded to the young Chinese waitress for another cup of coffee instead of the drink I really wanted. The Sunrise was licensed for beer and wine and both of them are for recreational drinkers. They take too long to come to the point, not unlike some people.

It seemed to me that it all boiled down to the one thing that people can't stand, in spite of The Aunts' good wishes, and that's to see two human beings just being happy together, taking care of each other, sticking up for each other and making the best of what there is on this short journey into the longest and greatest darkness of all. I'd heard the rumblings around the bar in The Blue Parrot. A lot of people seemed jealous of Pat and Lisa, wishing them to fail, as if that would confirm their own conviction that the game wasn't worth the candle and excuse them from the terrible burden of having to hope. What's sad isn't that there's so little in life to be happy about. It's that so many people settle for so much less.

Just at that moment, who should come in but the topics of conversation themselves. Things got too quiet too quickly, the way they always do in that situation, but they didn't seem to notice. At least, Lisa didn't. She was too excited. One of the female parrots had raked together a nest out of the wood shavings and paper strips they'd provided in the aviary and, miracle of miracles, laid an egg.

They'd been looking for me to celebrate. Pat ordered drinks all around, on him. The Aunts accepted glasses of white wine with girlish giggles, deliciously shocked by their own daring, drinking at such an hour. Old Al and I took him up on the beer. In my condition, it couldn't do any harm. Even Geoff accepted a beer. I overheard him and Pat quietly straightening things out on the sidelines after the toasts to the parrot.

"Sorry about yesterday, Geoff. I was out of line..."

"My fault, Pat. He was digging his grave with his mouth."

"I'll come around tomorrow and get you to even up this haircut. I feel like a car with two flat tires..."

The help was getting a little nervous, since nobody was ordering any food to go with these drinks, but Geoff was still the landlord so they didn't kick up. By the time I was working on my third beer, I was feeling almost human again and we had a pretty good party going on in back of the Sunrise. A few regulars from the barbershop filled out the crowd, drawn by the promise of a free drink or two.

I was glad Pat and Lisa were my friends, even though I knew

better. Friendship is more tragic than love because it lasts longer. It's odd how the most intimate of human relationships is also the most ephemeral and expendable. You can lose a wife, husband or lover and another one will always come along, someone to occupy that same passionate place in your life, making his or her predecessor a pleasant memory at best. But friends each have a unique no-deposit, no-return niche in your being, and if you lose a friend through accident, indifference or abuse, no one will ever quite fill that special emptiness or give you back that lost part of yourself.

The day was ending a lot better than it started. It could almost have passed for perfect, except that I had to go to work pretty soon.

"Come up to the Parrot," I said to Pat and Lisa, Old Al and Geoff and The Aunts, "I'll buy a round on the house."

I didn't make it a general announcement. Nobody needs that many friends.

Chapter 15

A day is never perfect until it's past. The best are the days you never suspect for a moment, the ones you never think might turn into memories. That way, you can't spoil them by crossing your fingers, touching wood or breaking your careless stride to skip cracks in the sidewalk. They're the days when you don't watch your step, mind your manners, your P's and Q's or your own business, when you mix your drinks and your metaphors and everything still turns out alright; the days when Murphy's Law is repealed and everything that can go wrong doesn't for a change.

We had our share of good days that summer, Pat and Lisa and Felix and I, days that flowed together to become a single memory; one image of afternoon sunlight filtered through the leaves of the overgrown apple and cherry trees in Pat's backyard, dappling the freshly cut grass whose smell made you want to lie down and roll in it, which only Felix had sense enough to do, and mingled with the scent of salmon or steaks sizzling on the grill and the earthy aroma of foil-wrapped potatoes baking in the coals. But the day I remember, the most perfect day of all, was the day we spent on Pat's boat, the re-christened "Lisa". Like the best and worst parties, it didn't start out with seating plans and engraved invitations.

Pat hadn't done much fishing that season. I didn't blame him. He had the best and most obvious reason in the world for sticking close. He still went down to the marina every day to work on the boat and pull the rag with his cronies on Float Five, but I thought it was mostly for the pleasure it gave him to know she was at home, waiting for him, at the end of the day or that she was having a glass of wine in The Blue Parrot, chatting with me until he joined us and took her off to go for chop suey at the Jasmine Inn.

Our day on the boat began on a hot Saturday night in the bar when Pat asked me to come down the next day and give him a hand installing a new generator on the diesel. Lisa said she'd come too, as long as we didn't plan to do any serious boating on the hated sea, and pack us a picnic lunch. She'd bring Felix and work on her tan while we worked on the engine. We'd have lunch, a few drinks and make a day of it.

It was Pat who suggested I bring somebody. I guess he figured I might be feeling like company around the two of them. In fact, I was. Without meaning to, lovers can make everybody else in the world feel like bit-players in the Christmas pageant. Lisa echoed Pat's suggestion with an enthusiasm that told me she was sure I wouldn't take him up on it. I've never met a woman yet who liked to share the limelight, or a man either, for that matter, but I wasn't sure I liked her being that confident about it.

I probably would've shrugged it off, but Helen came to the bar to order just then and, before I knew it, I'd asked her. It seemed like a good idea at the time. They both knew her and, if you got right down to it, my social life being what it was, there was nobody else I could've asked.

There may have been a full second of maidenly reticence before Helen said, "I'd love to. It sounds wonderful. My mother will take care of the girls. I'll make something for the picnic." And that was that. She was happier than a clam, but I've never been impressed by the emotive range of small bivalves.

Pat welcomed her to the fold with a broad grin. Despite Helen's offer to help with lunch, Lisa's smile was a little less certain. She looked like somebody who'd got more than they bargained for but wasn't sure she'd haggled hard enough over the price. I knew how she felt.

So, the next morning, which promised an even sunnier and hotter day, Helen met me at the old hotel with a basket bulging with food she must've stayed up half the night after her shift preparing. She was right on time, too.

My ex-wife was always precisely one half-hour late. That was just long enough for me to get pissed off, but not long enough for me to get righteously steamed. Of course, she was always very sorry and perfectly lovely when she did turn up, looking, as a Cran-Tini inspired advertising colleague once observed, "like she didn't have a pubic hair out of place." I didn't argue the point because I knew that whatever extra-marital activities she might engage in, her deeply rooted sense of priorities would never allow infidelity to interfere with grooming.

Sometimes I used to think about what I could have done with all those lost half-hours; found a cure for cancer, written a novel or two, developed a unified field theory, brought peace in our time. One thing I know for sure; when I punch my final time-card, it'll be too late to put in for the overtime then.

Helen and I strolled down to the marina under a sky as blue as forever. She looked good in shorts and sandals and one of those bright loose sun-tops. We smiled a lot at nothing in particular and didn't say much, as if not having the bar between us made us a little shy with each other. Out in the Inlet, sailors smoked over the fantails of anchored ships. A dark cormorant, it's long neck extended, swept low over the oily glistening sea like a living arrow. Flotillas of bufflehead ducks were working the shallows, their black and white heads popping up like tiny periscopes. I felt I could just walk on like that to anywhere. I didn't want anything, not even a drink.

We crossed the tracks near the mouth of the railroad tunnel that runs under the foot of Lonsdale Avenue. Just for something to say, I told Helen about when I was a bad kid, coming down to play on the wrong side of the tracks, how we used to wait for a train to come from the wheat pools east of Lonsdale, then we'd run into the tunnel from the west side, trying to beat the engine to the halfway point where there was a niche in the brick wall. Smaller than a confessional, a nest for rats and spiders, it was just deep enough to press ourselves flat into while the diesel deafened us and choked us with it's hot heavy breathing and the steel wheels spat sparks at us and screamed, threatening to make cripples of us all. Helen laughed nervously, listening to the dull throb of a distant engine, like a challenge, echoing from the far end of the tunnel.

"You wouldn't do that now, would you?" she teased, yet I had the feeling she was trying to prove something to herself; that she hadn't been wrong about me, that I wasn't as crazy as I let on, that underneath the cynical, saturated exterior there was a warm, wonderful and, above all, sensible human being. I couldn't disillusion her. It's hard to be honest with someone who wants to believe the best about you.

"No," I told her, "I wouldn't do that now," and let it go at that.

At the Mosquito Creek Marina, Float Five was where the workboats moored, the fishing vessels and small but powerful tuggers of the log-salvaging beachcombers. The other floats were flanked by fibreglass sloops and prestigious power cruisers, all bright paintwork and shiny stainless steel. Float Five looked like auction day at a bankrupt ships chandler. Frayed and dirty ropes and lines were coiled sloppily on decks or strewn with other well-worn gear across the floats to dry. Float Five stank of fish and wood, salt, grease, oil and sweat. A mangy black Lab who belonged to one of the beachcombers snarled at anything in top-siders or a yachting cap.

The dog thumped his tail lazily on the deck when Helen and I walked by. A couple of watchcaps and uncombed heads popped out of hatches and portholes. Behind us, there was a murmur and a low whistle or two at Helen's legs. I smiled to reassure her that the natives were friendly, but she knew how to take a salute.

Pat and Lisa were already aboard and a big enamel pot of coffee was simmering aromatically in the Lisa's tiny galley, for which I was grateful. Pat's coffee was strong enough to qualify for a Health Canada warning label, but it would jump-start your heart on the coldest morning and that's how it has to be if you're going to be out on the water at dawn. After a cup of that and a smoke, we got down to work and the girls got down to the essentials.

Under her top and shorts combination, Helen turned out to be wearing a yellow one-piece tank suit that flattered her by relieving any anxieties she might have about her waistline after two kids. There were a couple more discreet whistles of appreciation from adjacent boats, but when Lisa shucked her jeans and t-shirt, there was a silence on Float Five which can only be described as reverent.

That her dark blue bikini was conservative by contemporary standards only seemed to draw more attention to what it concealed. She was a decade, more or less, older than Helen and had a child of her own, she said, yet there was a feline grace about every curve and arch of her body that was so erotic it was almost abstract, impersonal, eternal. Like a classical statue, you could almost touch her with your eyes and she made your hands want to reach out, not in simple, trivial lust, but in awe and wonder. She was like the answer to a question you'd never found the words to ask.

"The only work done on Float Five today'll be done right here," Pat said quietly, smiling as we lowered ourselves into the engine hold.

"You got that right."

I was glad to get below deck. For a moment there, I'd been having what's known as second thoughts and those are usually enough trouble the first time around. I think it eased things between the girls, though. I knew Lisa well enough to figure she probably hadn't made an unselfconscious gesture since she was six years old. Though she gave no sign of it, she was acutely aware of the effect of her performance on the foredeck. The little cat-in-the-sun stretch with her eyes closed and the sun on her face, no hint of glamour-girl posing, was too perfect for her not to have known that she had the rapt attention of everyone in visual range and had eclipsed Helen as totally as the dark cold moon overshadows the sun.

It seemed to square things for whatever obscure jealousy she felt at Helen being there in the first place, because when Pat and I came up for beer two hours later, the generator successfully installed, you'd have sworn they were school-girl chums from the way the complimented each other's cooking as they stuffed us and Felix with fried chicken, hot biscuits and gravy, potato salad, coleslaw, curried eggs, fruit pies and cheese.

After lunch and a couple of stiff Kahlua and creams, Felix was too glutted to attempt anything more strenuous than stretching out on the cockpit in the shade of the radar scanner and eyeing the mangy Lab, who'd been trolling our gunwales for crumbs and hand-outs, both of them too hot, lazy and full to make something out of it. The girls repaired to the foredeck with a bottle of white wine to rub oil into each other's shoulders and exchange whispered feminine confidences. Pat and I lounged against the transom with our shirts off, smoking a couple of cheap cigars and getting into the rye and vodka respectively.

"There may be two luckier guys somewhere in the world," Pat remarked with a nod toward our voluptuously appointed forepeak, "But I'm damned if I can imagine who or where."

We drank to that. And to a few other things. Watching the sun turn tiny bits of debris and algae into motes of gold in the green water over the Lisa's port side, I couldn't think of a single place I'd rather be than right there with friends, a fine meal inside me, the sun on my chest, a glass in my hand, nothing to do and all day to do it.

As the sun took its afternoon mark and started its slow dive toward the snowcaps of Vancouver Island, hovering above the horizon haze like some cloud-borne Shangri-La, Felix roused himself and went dockside. Exploring the planks and pilings, sniffing and swatting at exposed mussels, he eventually settled himself at the wide gap where two floats were joined by short lengths of boom-chain. From there he could peer down at the minnows and sunfish perch that cluster and dart in the shadows under the floats.

Pat and I must've dropped into a light doze, but we both hit the deck fast when Lisa shrieked, "Felix!". She was standing in the bows, her hand up to her heart, out of shock or to hold up her untied top, bending over slightly to stare at the joint between the floats where Felix had been. I couldn't help noticing her bikini had ridden down on her hips an inch or two past the tan line. An angry snarl, that kind only a wet and frightened cat can crank out, erupted from under the forward float. Obviously unable to resist the lure of the minnows, Felix had tried his paw at fishing and fallen between the floats.

The soul of practicality, Helen stood up and re-fastened Lisa's top at the back. That seemed to calm her down, at least to the extent that she had the sense to re-arrange part two before we all got over the side and crowded around the opening between the floats.

"Try calling him," I suggested.

She tried. We all tried. And tried and tried. We could hear him and I could actually see a patch of wet black fur pressed up against the underside of the crack between the planks, about two feet past the junction. He was clinging to the curved side of the starboard log pontoon, getting wetter and not liking it one bit. There's a constant turbulence in every harbour, produced by tides and riptides, currents and the wash kicked up a thousand large and small craft. The floats were always in motion, pulled apart, slammed together, driven up and down, ground against each other, so the dimensions of the hole he'd fallen through kept changing, which may have put him off. Then too, he'd had one nasty shock at that particular opening. Either way, unhappy as he was, Felix wasn't moving.

Lisa gave me one of those looks women give men which say, "Do something!" more eloquently than words. As I wondered why the hell she was looking at me instead of Pat, I noticed he'd slipped back aboard the boat.

"Be careful," Helen whispered, as I handed her my drink and kicked off my shoes.

The water was stunningly, soberingly cold. I'd elected to dive. Though it took me deeper than I needed to go under the float, it seemed appropriate to the dramatic mood of the situation. When my eyes adjusted to the sting of salt water, I found myself in the weirdly echoing green world of the shallows, of old tires and bottles filled with sand, sunken dinghys and dead fish, half buried in the weeds where a million tiny scavengers scuttled. I made out the hull of the Lisa to my right and, above, a strip of shadow under the floats. I came up between the pontoons, face to face with Felix.

"Hello, tuna-breath," I gasped, spitting salt and gripping a slimy log.

He growled miserably and hissed at me. I was cold and frightened there in the dirty water. I could feel the tiny ragged claws clicking in expectation as the weeds wrapped themselves around my desperately treading ankles. I cuffed Felix across the head and grabbed the scruff of his neck in one motion. I had to hold tight. He was only stunned for a second, then I had a handful of wet, squirming, angry and terrified cat. But before he could rake me, I shoved him up through the hole into Lisa's waiting arms. As I sank out of sight, the floats slammed together with an ominous thump.

I swam underwater a couple of yards to clear the float and came up in the channel on the opposite side from where the Lisa was moored. Instead of a hero's welcome, I surfaced to stare into the suddenly horrified face of a young speedboat jockey who was entering the slipway much too fast. His steel bow-line ring was about six feet from my head and getting bigger by the split second. I dropped down and back, sinking for all I was worth and silently cursing the human body's natural bouyancy and noticing with a peculiar calm that his hull could do with a scrape, as I watched the inexorable progress of the frothing prop toward my throat. Deafened by the engine, I felt the blades whirl through my drifting hair.

When I re-surfaced and crawled up onto the float, helped by Lisa and Helen, the speedboat was already against the dock and the guy was striding angrily toward me, followed by a couple of his buddies. Their girlfriends in the boat looked very nervous.

"You fuckin'..."

He got that far when Pat got in his way.

"There's a sign on the piling at the end of the wharf says you're to Reduce Speed and Leave No Wash, son." With his free hand, pointed to the wake that was still bouncing half the boats in the marina around like corks. From his other hand, a crowbar dangled as casually as a crowbar can dangle in that kind of situation. I found out later he'd gone back aboard the Lisa to get it so he could pry up the plank Felix was under.

There were three of them and for a minute it looked like trouble. I was too busy spewing up half the Inlet to be any use. Then the boys realized they were on Float Five, surrounded by a growing and hostile crowd of fishermen and beachcombers, as ratty a mob as ever gutted a dogfish. Suddenly they were more scared than mad. The mouthy one promised to pay closer attention to M.O.T. regulations in future and they were allowed to retreat to the bright shiny speedboat. They were in the wrong channel anyway.

We called it a day, too. Felix went home in Lisa's arms, wrapped in a towel, and Helen insisted they drop me at her place to warm up, even though it was still hot enough that I'd almost dried out by the time we got there.

The kitchen of the townhouse duplex where she lived was decorated with fingerpaintings and drawings, each crudely signed by her daughters. With a towel over her shoulder, she led me to the bedroom, ordering me to take off my jeans and shorts to let them dry. After the fiasco with Marion, I was in no mood to make a fool of myself again so soon, nor did I want my body making promises to Helen that my heart couldn't keep. I started to mumble the coward's litany of improvised excuses.

"Hush," she said, as she peeled off my things and sat me on the edge of the bed, "It's alright now."

She took off her own suit with motions that were as unintentionally erotic as they were deliberately unseductive. It was like watching your wife undress for bed or soap herself in the bath. The only thing hard about me was the lump in my throat.

Then she towelled my damp head , standing so close I could smell the sun and oil, heat and creosote clinging to her skin and everything really was alright.

"Light chop with a small craft warning," I muttered as we toppled backward into the queen-size waterbed, bobbing like bottles with fading desperate messages inside. A back-eddy dropped me into a less than suave pool in the approximate centre. "Have you got life-jackets for this thing?" I said, raising my hand like a drowning man going down. She put her arms around my neck.

"I'll save you," she said.

"I'll only drag you down with me," I replied, planting a slippery kiss on her nose instead of her mouth, thanks to an unpredictable ripple under the sheets.

But it was still alright a couple of hours later, with both of us half-asleep and the red glow of sunset on the wall of the bedroom.

"What about the girls?" I asked during a lull in the proceedings.

"They're spending the night at my mom's," she whispered with what I took to be a satisfied sigh. The Russians had the right idea. With women Admirals, I mean. When it comes to foresight and logistical planning, they're unbeatable.

It had been a very full day, as close to perfect as they come. I'd done a favour for a friend, got my hands righteously dirty, enjoyed the sun and good food and company, performed a daring rescue, even if it was only a drunk cat, narrowly escaped death or serious maiming and made evidently satisfactory love to a woman. And I hadn't heard a word about parrots all day.

In spite of my reservations about staying under other people's roofs, I could feel myself pulled down by the irresistible undertow of sleep. It's amazing, sometimes, how all the cold questions and colder answers , the whole permanently frozen icecap of pain and loneliness, can melt against the simple warmth of a sleeping woman's back.

Chapter 16

I woke up very early the next morning. Even more unusual was the circumstance that I was lying, or floating, to be precise, in a strange bed in a strange room beside a woman who was still a stranger, though I'd worked with her for about a year and knew as much about her, her children, her hopes and dreams and troubles, as I knew about anybody.

Maybe it was just the room. I woke up looking at the ceiling, one of those stipple plastered apartment ceilings which are a magnet for dust, impossible to clean and a bitch to paint.I remember thinking it was much too low. I knew I'd had dreams I couldn't remember at first, except for a general oppressiveness, and I wondered if that had anything to do with it. My dreams were used to plenty of overhead space to dissipate in like steam.

Or it could have been the water-bed. I remembered then that I'd dreamt of drowning, of being in the dark water in the shadow of the hull of a big ship in the harbour, knowing that only a few feet above there was sunlight and fresh air and sailboats filled with happy people rubbing sunscreen on each other. Frantically kicking away from the weedy barnacled hull, I'd watched as the propeller scythed the oddly silent water with huge brass blades, sucking me into its vortex while the mud below seethed with tiny crabs barely able to support the weight of their enormous claws. I wanted to get out of that bed.

The Blue Parrot

Shifting my hip onto the edge of the heavy mock-Spanish burnt-wood frame that seems to contain most of these dry lakes of the Seventies, I managed to crawl ashore without creating enough turbulence to wake Helen. The tops of the grain elevators filled part of the bedroom window, cutting off most of the view of the harbour and the city beyond, and I remembered I'd dreamed of trains as well.

Helen lived on a bluff directly overlooking the tracks and the coupling and uncoupling of cars, like a string of explosions as they slammed together along the line, and the constant rumble of the diesels must've penetrated my sleep. No wonder I'd dreamed of the tunnel I'd told her about. Only in the dream, the tunnel seemed to go on forever in subterranean darkness, lit only by the glare of an approaching engine I couldn't outrun. Rats squealed under my feet, scampering along the vibrating rails. I was running out of breath and I couldn't find the niche in the wall, the small dark space I could squeeze myself into and be safe from the maiming wheels. I'd forgotten where it was.

Helen had done something with my clothes, put them somewhere to dry. I didn't like creeping around other peoples houses at the best of times and naked I liked it even less. I felt like an indecent housebreaker. It reminded me of the times when I'd gone along on break-and-enter expeditions, B'n'E's, we called them, when I was a teenager. There was that alien silence, the smell of a strange house, empty rooms filled with other people's possessions left trustingly where they'd put them down; a cold half cup of scummy coffee on the sideboard, stale butts in an ashtray, unfamiliar furniture, photographs of strangers on the walls, Kodak *lares et penates*, things that were like clues in a mystery. I'd gone along for the adventure, not loot, but it made me feel haunted somehow, like an archaeologist must feel in an ancient tomb, and I gave up my dream of becoming a famous cat-burglar and jewel thief.

I found my pants, shorts and shirt hung neatly over the backs of chairs at the kitchen table. I'd no sooner made myself decent than Helen came in, tying a slightly frayed blue terrycloth robe around her, looking good for a woman with her hair askew and her face still in the makeup bag. She walked into my arms as naturally as sunrise. I hugged her quickly and turned away.

"Your husband's a damn fool," I muttered, stepping back into my own still slightly damp shoes.

She put her hand on her hip with a wry smirk. "If he is, what are you?"

"A bigger one?" I admitted with a laugh. She knew I'd've been gone like a dawn breeze in a minute more. "You're pretty sharp early in the morning."

"What do you want for breakfast?" she asked with a sly grin.

I slumped into a chair. "There's no such meal as breakfast," I said, "Life begins at lunch."

"Try living with two little girls who have to get ready for school and kindergarten for a week or two," she replied, cracking eggs into a bowl, "You'll believe in breakfast, the Tooth Fairy, the Easter Bunny, Santa Claus, Sailor Moon, Power Rangers, aliens in UFOs, mutants, Cinderella, Beauty and the Beast..."

"I believe in all of them," I said, "It's everything else, the customers in the bar every night, for instance, that I have trouble believing in."

With the sun coming in from the front room, reaching into the cool kitchen and spilling across the linoleum like a puddle of melting gold, and Helen standing at the stove, scrambling eggs with a fork while the butter whispered in the pan, the bittersweet scent of coffee drifting from the pot, the calendars and kids' drawings and sports day ribbons decking the walls like domestic icons, I could almost have taken her up on it. I had that lump in my throat, the one that felt like I was trying to swallow my own shrivelled heart. I wanted to run down the alley, vaulting over bikes and wagons, through the skin-shredding salmonberry and bindweed thickets, to the oily stinking waterfront where I could sit alone on a rotting log among the rats and wild cats and smoke my last bitter cigarette on an empty stomach before I stumbled back to my tall, silent safe rented room with the bottle of vodka in the cooler under the bed.

Like most wives, Helen was telepathic. "There's some tomato

juice in the fridge," she said, "You're lucky the girls don't like it. There's a lemon in there too, if it hasn't dried out, and you'll find a mickey of vodka in the freezer. You could make us a couple of Marys."

God help us if we ever get women Generals. Like a dutiful trooper, I went into action. I managed to find suitable glasses without having to ask. In the military, that's what they call initiative. In my case, a rare moment of real motivation.

Scrambled eggs, bacon, toast, Bloody Marys and coffee. Helen's kitchen was starting to feel dangerously like home. Worse, it was starting to feel like home had never felt. It occurred to me that, somewhere across town, my ex-wife was probably stuffing a croissant filled with smoked salmon and goat-cheese into the face of some Porsche jockey who was rinsing it down with a Mimosa of champagne and orange juice. If the hangover didn't get him, the indigestion would. I wouldn't have traded places with him or anybody else, which brought up a subject that had been lurking in the back of my mind like a rogue rat in a cheddar warehouse.

"What about your husband?" I asked.

"What about him?" she challenged.

"Is he likely to drop in for coffee?"

It wasn't that I was particularly afraid of a punch-up. I just feel that I fight better when I'm in the right and, having slept with another man's wife, in his bed, under a roof he paid rent on, however sporadically, I was uneasily aware that there wasn't enough ground under my feet for a toe-hold, never mind a place to make a stand.

"He won't be back 'til he runs out of money," she replied, matter-of-factly, "Or girls who'll lend it to him."

"What about your girls?"

"My Mom'll get them off to school and bring them home for lunch," she said patiently.

I nodded. "Okay. I just don't think breakfast is a good time to be introduced to young ladies. I'd rather not be known as The Man Who Sleeps With Mommy."

Helen smiled. She knew I was weasling furiously, looking for a right way to be gone, out of her comfortable kitchen, out of her uncomfortable life.

"What are you so worried about?" she asked gently.

"Well, you're married..."

"You call this married?" she said with a rueful smile.

"You never know how married you are until you think about getting unmarried," I said with a wisdom as deep as two Bloody Marys.

Helen unbelted her robe and stood up. That was so unexpectedly and profoundly distracting, I had to take a tighter grip on my drink.

"Are you coming peaceably, or do I have to drag you?" she asked with a coy smile.

"Helen..." I stammered, like a man who's torn up his speech for dramatic effect and finds he has nothing to say.

The robe floated down to form a blue puddle around her feet. She grinned at me like a truant schoolgirl undressing for her boyfriend while the parents were out. I came peaceably.

Women think men's brains are located directly below their belt-buckles. There's a lot of circumstantial evidence to support that conclusion, but it's a hell of a way to get the last word in a discussion. Maybe she realized it wasn't so much her as the setting, her cosy lived-in kitchen, that set me off. I'd never made love with my ex-wife in the kitchen. Never even thought of it. Among all those German knives, Swedish crystal glasses, Italian designer pastel plates, immaculate food processors, microwaves, electric coffee grinders and garlic presses, it would have been like having sex during a meeting of the General Assembly of the United Nations.

Later, trying to shave with Helen's ergonomically curved pink plastic disposable razor, I felt like one of the boys. On the buses, you can always tell which guys got lucky and didn't make it home last night. They're the ones with little bits of tissue stuck to their faces to blot the nicks inflicted by borrowed razors normally used for shaving ladies' legs and underarms.

It's not easy, shaving in someone else's bathroom. The mirror is always too big or too small, and not where you're used to seeing yourself. In Helen's place, it covered the whole width of the wall above the sink and cabinets. I hadn't seen so much of myself in years and it made me a bit uneasy, the way you feel in a very small room with a stranger. Usually, I shaved in the shower without a mirror. I discovered you never cut yourself if you don't look at your face. I can't explain it, but it works, which puts it in the same category as most things in life.

Helen was dressed by the time I'd survived the Death of A Thousand Cuts.

"I called my Mom," she said, "She's going to pick up the girls from school and bring them home for lunch, if you'd like to hang around and meet them."

I was guiltily grateful it was September and the kids were back in classrooms. She didn't know I had a little girl of my own out there, in her special classroom, learning to communicate and make her way in a silent world, and there wasn't enough vodka left in the mickey to make me go through all that again.

"I'd like to, some other time," I mumbled, "But I've got to run."

"Ever going to stop?" she asked gently, with that slow understanding and inviting smile.

She didn't have my number yet, but she was counting fast. Another breakfast or two with her and I'd find a Bloody Mary set-up on the table beside a fresh pack of my brand of smokes and the paper folded back to the Careers section, a freshly ironed shirt and slacks over the back of the chair, a pot of coffee in the thermos and my filled lunchbox beside the kids. She still looked good, even in the sweatshirt and jeans she'd pulled on, and if she'd fixed her face and hair it'd been no more than a quick scrape and comb at the bedroom dresser mirror while I was trying not to cut my throat in the bathroom.

My ex used to get up at least an hour before I did and lock herself in the bathroom with a carafe of French Roast, the radio and two makeup bags the size of expedition knapsacks. I never could understand how she could be incapable of talking to me until the ritual was complete, yet she could listen to the manic morning deejays babbling out bad news from all over the world, interrupted by bursts of insufferably bouncy morning music or, worse, those call-in talk radio shows that give freedom of speech a bad name.

"I guess my legs'll give out eventually and they'll drag me down," I said, with a rueful smile of my own, "Although, when I look at Old Al, I wonder..."

"Is that what you want to become?" she asked quietly, "An old man living in one room in an old hotel?"

"Well, I'm halfway there," I answered with a hollow chuckle, "All I have to do now is get older and I'm taking that one day at a time."

I used to think getting older was just a matter of patience and reasonably good luck. The longer I live, the more it seems like a full time job. By the time I got to the end of the block, I felt a lot older and already homesick for Helen's kitchen. I was heading back to my room in the old hotel, but I wasn't going home. I didn't know where home was.

I knew the feeling would pass. Home isn't a place, anyway. It's more like a memory of childhood we try to re-create in a changed world. Those who remember the past, those who really learn the lessons of history, are the ones who are condemned to repeat it; to imitate their loving or abusive parents, to become their fathers and marry their mothers, to be always searching for that lost Home in the real estate Multiple Listings and mortgaging their disinherited souls to buy it back, forever moving into bigger houses in better neighbourhoods, until the kids are suddenly grown and gone and the process reverses itself in a shrinking succession of townhouses, apartments, senior citizens housing projects and nursing homes staffed by strangers.

Though she wouldn't have thought of it that way, I knew that was what Helen wanted. For now all she wanted was to move her girls out of the rough, rented neighbourhood of the waterfront into a house up the hill with a picket fence and enough yard for a garden and some grass for the girls and maybe a little dog, near schools where the kids didn't learn to talk like truckers, at least until puberty. Instead of slinging drinks in a losers' lounge, getting her ass grabbed by sailors and putting down slurred propositions, she wanted to cook dinner every afternoon in a cockroach-free kitchen for a man who was going to come in at the same time every evening, kiss her cheek, slap her gently on the fanny and tell her she smelled almost as good as her cooking.

I didn't blame her for that, but I couldn't figure why she'd hit on me, of all people. She wanted something worlds away from what Marion had wanted and both of them had a wrong number. I couldn't be Helen's knight in teflon armour any more than I could be Marion's male whore. It would have been easier to satisfy Marion. At best, that would have been one bad memory, forgotten as fast as a hangover. Helen wanted a lifetime, and maybe she was entitled to one, but not to mine.

On the face of it, you have to wonder why anybody drinks in a bar. I mean, it's safer, cheaper and more comfortable to drink at home. You can choose the company and the music, there's no such thing as closing time and nobody's going to pull you over and make you walk the white line and blow up the balloon on the way from the living room to your bedroom. Yet, every night, millions of people go out to dark and dirty bars filled with unpredictable strangers where the music is lousy and too loud, to pay too much money for too many short-poured drinks and tell people they don't know, things they wouldn't tell their spouses or best friends.

The only reason I can think of is that there are times when you can't look at anything in your own home without thinking about how much it cost you, how much of your brief time on earth you traded, to get the money to pay for it, or how much of your pride or somebody else's shit you swallowed to apply for the loan. Even blank walls can remind you of the interest rate on your mortgage.

In a bar, you own nothing and owe nothing except the bottom line on your tab. If you want to sit there all night without saying a word more than it takes to order, no one will accuse you of being moody or anti-social. But if you want to talk, there's always somebody who wants to talk as badly as you do, or even just to listen to the sound of another human voice, as long as it's ordering a round. A bar is a true democracy. There's one law for the rich or poor and that's the price of beer or highballs and even tips can't amend it because any bartender or cab driver knows the poor tip better. They have less respect for money because they know how little it will buy.

I did have a home, in a way. As I got ready to start my shift, I realized I'd come to think of Pat's place as a kind of home. He'd taken in Lisa and Felix, given them safe harbour, but he'd also taken in more of me than I liked to admit to myself. They were the closest thing I had to family, not a very ordinary family maybe, but what with everybody else having ex-husbands, ex-wives, partial custody of children by assorted spouses and putative parents and so on, these days, maybe not so odd after all.

I was glad Pat and Lisa dropped in for a drink that night, so glad I almost wished Helen was working. It was just as well she wasn't. I'd only have had a few too many shots of frozen vodka and thawed out enough to say something she'd have regretted for the rest of her life.

Pat told me what a fine girl Helen was and Lisa avidly seconded the motion. I made it unanimous, voting Marion's proxy, since she was still bitchily avoiding the bar except out of necessity. The only one of us she had any time for was Felix and he was getting happily half-shot down by my ankles. He'd forgiven me for rescuing him, like a drunk who forgives his favourite bartender for cutting him off and giving him the rush when he's been drinking out of his depth. We drank to Helen and to the unhatched egg brooding in the aviary up at Pat's. I looked over my raised glass at the old blue neon parrot outlined against the circle of infinite darkness and wondered what would become of us all.

Chapter 17

I hadn't seen Pat and Lisa in a week or so and I felt thoroughly fit and able to withstand another bout of Parrot Fever when Pat came in, in the middle of a slow shift, looking like he had something a lot worse. He came straight to the bar like it was a barricade he meant to storm.

"Have you seen Lisa?" he demanded.

I shook my head honestly. "Not since I saw you last." The fight went out of him in a sigh as he sagged onto one of the imitation bamboo barstools. "You better pour us both one," he said with something like a groan.

I did, topping off a large one for myself. Pat pinned a folded fifty to the bar like a butterfly with the point of his clasp knife. There were a lot of drinks in that bill and it was nowhere near closing time. The knife gave us space to talk; the few customers at the bar moved discreetly to tables further away in the deeper, safer shadows.

"What's up, Pat?"

He took a pull on his rye and seven like he'd been on desert march with Moses. "She's gone," he said at last, "Lisa's gone."

I rolled with it. "Are you sure?" I asked, "I mean, women have kind of a flexible sense of time, you know..."

I was just trying to get the facts before I got the shakes. He shook his head, almost smiling at the thin straw I'd tossed him to clutch.

"She's gone, alright," he said, "I think she took the cat and a couple of the birds."

"You think?"

A challenging look, the sudden spooky belligerence of the unpredictable drunk, took over his face. "You ever try to count that many parrots while they're all flapping and climbing around, squawking 'I love you, Lisa' to beat hell?" he demanded in a not so dull roar.

I admitted I never had.

"Well, okay, then...."

He drained his glass as though winning that one entitled him to a free drink. I set him up again and sucked the top inch off my glass.

"I tried to count 'em," he said, shaking his head wearily. "I've been tryin' to count 'em for two days. That's how long she's been gone. Two goddamn days."

His eyes looked like a map of secondary roads etched in red.

"Been having a few shots to calm your nerves, Pat?" I asked blandly.

"What if I have?" he answered with a shrug. "Christ, I needed it, trying to count those damn birds. I'd have a belt and count 'em. Then I'd have another and count 'em again...And every time I'd come up with a different number. I never got the same number twice. There's supposed to be sixteen parrots in there and I came up with every number but...Fifteen, fourteen, seventeen. I even got twenty once. I'm sure she took a couple of them damn birds..."

I wanted to get his mind off the parrots. It didn't seem to be getting him anywhere in a direction nobody in his right mind could go. And I wasn't getting any closer to finding out why Lisa had left if, in fact, she had.

"Pat, I'm flying on instruments here. Why don't we get some altitude and a bit of an overview. I'm lost, so let's start by backing up to where it made sense."

"It doesn't make any sense....None of it makes any sense," he said thickly.

"I'll drink to that," I said, "But suppose we start with what happened two days ago."

He took his time, like a diver coming up from deep water, wary of the bends.

"Well....We had some people drop in...Rick and some of his friends...Boys and girls...They're just kids..."

I'd met Rick, Pat's surviving son, a couple of times. About twenty, he was tall and languidly lanky and well aware that he was good looking in an angular, androgynous way; the sort of kid who admires his own bone-structure. He had large liquid eyes and such a laid-back air about him that it was hard to take it personally when he barely acknowledged my existence. He was simply too world-weary to give me the attention I no doubt deserved. Even his voice was an exhausted drawl.

I'd disliked him immediately, which he sensed and somehow, by taking such marginal note of it, managed to make it rebound, as though it said more about me than about him. Maybe it did. I disliked him because he patronized his father, treating Pat with a veil of politeness too thin to mask the underlying contempt. I'm sure it wasn't entirely his fault. He'd reached the age where he knew everything; he just hadn't yet discovered how little that is.

"So?..." I said, like a stage prompter.

Pat shrugged and tapped his empty glass. The fifty was still pinned to the bar, so I filled it for him, but I took a deep breath, pulled the knife out of the bar and folded it, returning it to him with his change. He pocketed it with a vaguely apologetic grunt.

"We had sort of a party..."

I could imagine. Rich and his equally *weltschmertz* pals, all waiters and busboys disguised as art students and musicians and their silent girlfriends who are probably pretty enough under the vampire makeup but radiate a sexual angst out of proportion to their years, all sitting around sucking up the old man's booze, talking over his smiling head in their private coded language of fashion, charming his lady friend with their youthful cynicism and cruel wit.

"What happened then?"

125

"They really liked the parrots, y'know...And they played some music..Not my kind of stuff...After a while, they all decided to go to some dance club..."

"And?"

He gave me a sheepish look. "I guess I can't blame Lisa for wanting to go with them," he said, "She doesn't get out to that kind of thing with an old bird like me..."

"But she hasn't been home since?" I finished for him.

He nodded grimly.

"I think she came back last night," he said, "While I was out looking for her. I went to a few of those clubs, where my son goes. They're kind of strange, y'know? Dark, painted black inside and nobody seems to be having a very good time..."

"I know," I said, "When you're young, being conspicuously happy is a form of indecent exposure."

Ignoring my attempt to lighten up, he plowed on. "Anyway, when I got back, I was sure she'd been there. Some of her things are gone. Just clothes and things. She never took anything that wasn't hers...but I haven't seen Felix around either and she wouldn't leave without him, would she?...Then I started looking at the birds and I'm sure there aren't as many as there was...I know she took a couple of 'em with her. If I could just..."

"Pat," I interrupted, "Forget the fucking birds for a minute. Did you call your son?"

He nodded. "I called him yesterday. All day. I finally got him."

"What'd he say?"

"He said he was sorry."

I cocked an eyebrow. "That's all? Did he say what he was sorry about, exactly?"

Shaking his head slowly, Pat drained his drink and pushed the empty forward for a reload. "He just said he was sorry and hung up. I tried to call him back, but there's been no answer ever since. The phone company says he might've unplugged his phone."

"You swing by his place last night?" I asked casually.

He nodded, looking even more sheepish. "I was gonna go up and knock. There was a light on, but...I felt kinda sick, y'know?"

I knew. For making you feel horrible, sick, terrified and ridiculous all at the same time, love is hard to beat.

"Rick and Lisa seemed to get along pretty well together, did they?" I inquired blandly.

Pat nodded reluctantly. "Yeah, I guess so. She sat beside him on the couch all the time, just listening to him. I couldn't get a word in. Maybe I thought it was a little funny, but I'd had a few drinks and I wanted them to like each other."

"Sounds like they did."

"Yeah," he said thickly, "But I just don't understand it...It doesn't make sense..."

"Pat," I said, helping myself to another shot, "The list of things that don't make sense gets longer every millisecond."

Shaking his head, he said, "You don't understand," desperately, as if something was bursting inside him, "Last year...Rick....My son...He told me he was...gay....Y'know?"

He had me cold with that one. When you can't think of anything to say, it's time for a very big drink. I had one and built another. I figured I was going to need it.

"You got to help me.." he muttered.

"I don't see what I can do, Pat...Honestly..."

"You got to help me count those parrots," he insisted, "If I can just find out how many there are...If there's two missing... I'll know."

He was strung tighter than barbed wire, trying to make sense out of the senseless.

"Alright, alright," I said, with a feeling already well and truly sunk, "I'll come up after work and see what I can do."

He lapsed into silence at the end of the bar near the wall, raising his glass from time to time for a reload. Nobody bothered him. The Aunts polished off the shots of Henkes Apricot Brandy they were treating themselves to after their weekly dinner out at the Jasmine. They gave Pat three long and curious looks, accompanied by some church-whispering. Old Al took one look at him, shook his head and took his rum off to join the corner booth philosophers who were fine-tuning their plan to restructure the Canadian economy so the working man could get some justice in this world. I went drink for drink with Pat the whole way, until the first fifty and the best part of another were nothing but damp change in the tip jar, wondering what the hell I was going to do with him later.

Once, when he was in the can pumping his bilges, Marion came to the bar for an order. She'd been avoiding us both all night, but this time her face made no attempt to hide the fact that she knew what was going on.

"Marion, please," I said, "Don't say, I hate to say I told you so..."

"I won't," she replied through a hideously forced smile, "I don't hate to say it...I told you so."

I shook my head, lit a smoke and emptied my glass in one long cold swallow that left me feeling like somebody had just split my head with an axe.

At closing time we took a cab to Pat's. Neither of us was in any shape to drive his car and I'd picked up a crock from the bar. The place was a sty. Empty glasses and bottles and full ashtrays decorated every room. A couple of congealed half-eaten meals festered on the kitchen sideboards. There was a sharp tangy smell of droppings from the uncleaned aviary.

The birds were nervous, even though it was night and dim in the large cage. They shifted restlessly from perch to perch, squawking horrendously from time to time, "I love you, Lisa...I love you Lisa..."

"You see what I mean?" Pat demanded belligerently, "They want to know where she is. I can't do anything with them...I can't stand it. They do it all night and I can't sleep. I can't even count them...I just can't stand it..."

"Have they got food and water?" I asked, peering into the aviary, my presence provoking a chorus of squawks and flappings.

"I guess so," Pat said absently, "Enough for a couple of days."

"It's been a couple of days," I remarked, trying to be practical,

"And the aviary needs to be cleaned."

"Fuck it," Pat snapped.

That was final enough to discourage argument. I didn't want to go in there any more than he did.

"She has to come back," he insisted, "She has to take care of the birds, doesn't she?"

I didn't have an answer for that.

"Help me," he mumbled, stumbling over to the aviary, "Help me count 'em. Then I'll know for sure..."

I started counting. What else was I supposed to do? It didn't take me long to appreciate what he'd been up against. I counted the moving birds half a dozen times and actually came up with sixteen twice, though I got a different number both times when I tried to repeat the feat. Pat was pacing, or trying to, since he was getting noticeably unsteady on his pins. He wasn't having any better luck counting and he wasn't taking my word for anything.

I couldn't see the point. He'd already showed me the empty drawer and closet that had held most of Lisa's clothes and things. Felix was nowhere to be seen. It all seemed pretty obvious to me. It even made a weird kind of sense, but I wouldn't have been able to explain it to Pat.

How could I tell him that for Lisa, his son Rick was what she had been for him? Younger, emotionally confused, sexually vulnerable; someone who not only seemed to need her but who could give her back one last fresh taste of her own vanishing youth? How could I make him understand that some people don't want to be happy? That their unhappiness is their most precious possession, the one thing they'll never forgive you for taking from them? That being "Poor Lisa" or whoever is exactly who they want to be; that their hard luck story and the sympathy it gets them is their back-stage pass through a life they haven't the courage or faith enough to face without the lies they tell themselves and everyone else?

Counting the screeching parrots, as they squeaked "I love you, Lisa" I could have hated her then, in my small disengaged way, but I didn't have time. I had my hands full trying to talk Pat out of killing them all. He was getting mean and incoherent, rambling about going into the aviary and twisting the heads off each and every one of the fuckers and laying them out in a row to count them once and for all. "Then I'll know for sure..." he burbled, nodding over his rye.

It took me about two hours of steady drinking to change the subject. By that time the birds had settled down a bit and the sky was getting thin and pale over the mountains. Out in the harbour it was low slack tide, the hour when life is at its low ebb and the souls of the frail stumble out to book passage with the ferryman. I was worn out, blind drunk, fed up and fucked up, though not too far from home. I almost passed out on the couch, but between the booze and the birdshit stink, I thought a walk in the dawn air couldn't do me anything but good. I heaved Pat onto his lonely bed, dropped his suspenders, pulled off his boots and covered him with a spare blanket. He was snoring before I was done.

I let myself out the back way and staggered across the yard, trying to get away from myself, which is one escape not even the Great Houdini could pull off. I didn't hate Lisa for what she'd done and and I didn't hate Pat for being fool enough to fall in love with her, but I hated myself for having hoped for them.

I had hoped for them with the hopeless hope of longshot horse-players howling themselves hoarse for a spavined hack who trails the field, running not to win but just to stay one frantic furlong farther from the pet food factory. I had hoped for them as you hope for has been heavyweights who give away two decades to murderous young punchers and still fight and fight on, trying to win back just one more rubber-legged round from punchdrunk oblivion.

I looked for Felix. The barbecue was a pile of blackened bricks, like a stone hearth that survives a house burned to the ground. There was nothing on the branches of the trees but leaves waiting to fall. The alley looked like the end of the world.

Chapter 18

I read about it in the morning paper one afternoon a few days later. It was one of those one-paragraph, single-column stories staff reporters without bylines cut their canine teeth on. Man Kills Parrots. Charges Pressed. Cruelty to Animals Alleged. Neighbours heard horrific noises and called police. The defendant appeared in Magistrate's Court, bandaged and stitched from the Emergency Ward as a result of scratches and bites inflicted by the terrified, doomed birds. The kind of thing you skim-read on the bus and shake your head at how incomprehensibly weird and cruel people are.

You have your problems; your mortgage coming up for renewal, your delinquent kids, your wife whacked out on vodka and Valium, your tar-pit affair with the secretary in Payroll, but at least they're the normal problems of the real world. For a moment, reading, you are exposed to irrational grief, inexplicable pain, brutal revenge. You fold the paper, get off at your usual stop, go to work and forget the story before coffee-break.

The reporter hasn't got the story, of course. Reporters almost never do, being too busy getting the facts. One day, when I was a reporter myself, I hung up the phone after calling a woman to ask how she felt about her teenage daughter being raped and strangled and mutilated a few days before. By the time I finished writing her annoyingly incoherent responses into coherent copy, I wasn't frustrated or pissed off anymore. I handed in my resignation with the story.

    After I read the paper, I walked up to Pat's place, but I knew there was nobody home before I knocked on the door. The house had that quiet haunted look of sudden abandonment. A neighbour peered over the fence, drawn by my presence in the yard of the suddenly infamous house.

    "He's gone," she said, in her smug old woman's voice, "On his boat. He's a fisherman, you know."

    "I know," I said.

    She waited a moment.

    "It was terrible," she confided, "I've never heard anything so horrible in all my..."

    "Fuck off," I said, loud enough to stop her cold.

    "I beg your pardon?" she squeaked.

    I said, "Fuck off," a lot louder.

    "Well!...I'll...I'll get my husband, you..."

    "I'll only tell him to fuck off, too," I warned her.

    I walked around the house. Pat was right. It was uncanny how fast an uninhabited house began to look like one. The unemptied garbage can bulged and buzzed with flies in the shadows under the sundeck where Lisa and I almost minutely altered the course of history. Empty bottles lay half-submerged in the uncut grass.

    I didn't go up to the sundeck. I figured the SPCA or the RCMP had cleaned up the mess in the aviary and the poor dead parrots were in a cold locker somewhere, properly tagged and counted at last, waiting to be used in evidence at Pat's trial. I wondered briefly what they did with that solitary unhatched egg. I didn't want to see the aviary anyway. I wasn't that ghoulish and I figured the nosy neighbour was probably giving guided tours five minutes after the last cop car pulled away.

    I'd come by to see if there was anything I could do for Pat. Maybe I felt guilty for not having stayed with him, knowing what kind of shape he was in, but I couldn't have babysat him around the clock and I couldn't have prevented him from doing what he did. There wasn't much I could do for him now, except hold his coat while they ganged-up on him, but that's what friends are for. If he'd been released on bail and gone out on the boat to get away from it all, it would probably be the best thing for him, I thought.

Around the front of the house again, I sat on the steps and had a smoke in the sun. I had most of the afternoon to kill before my shift. I was deciding where I could get a good big Bloody Mary for breakfast when I realized I wasn't alone. Peeking around the corner of the three concrete steps, almost hidden in the low juniper shrubs, was a small dirty white mask.

"Felix," I said. I wasn't calling him; just saying his name to make sure he was real.

He emerged from the bushes, thin and grubby from living out of garbage cans again and meowed demandingly. Suddenly, I was enraged. Jumping up, I aimed a kick at him that missed by a country kilometer.

"Get lost, you black bad luck bastard!" I snarled, "Find somebody else to jinx! Or do the world a favour and get squashed by a garbage truck!"

He disappeared into the shrubs so fast I wasn't sure I'd seen him. I trotted up the walk to the street and began striding away from the house as fast as I could without breaking into a sprint.

I needed to get something into my stomach, if only so I'd have something to throw up. About two houses down, I made the same mistake as Lot's wife. Glancing over my shoulder, I saw Felix sitting on the sidewalk in front of Pat's, his head down morosely, looking after me. He let out a low awful howl, the kind you hear when cats fight or make love.

I turned around and started walking slowly back toward him. He didn't back off. I could have kicked him the length of the block and he had every reason to suppose I would. Kneeling down, I rubbed his dusty head. A fresh cut oozed behind his left ear, still sticky with blood congealed in the fur. He meowed once more, mournfully.

"I know," I said, "She even left you." I looked the cut over more closely. "What's this? You losing your moves? Getting too old and slow for the cat racket? That's the trouble, boy...The dogs just keep getting bigger and faster...C'mon. I'll buy you a drink."

He sagged in my arms, worn out from fending for himself for most of a week. I carried him back to the old hotel, put him on my bed and got the day shift barman to front me a double Bloody and a double Kahlua and cream on the cuff. We both felt a little better after breakfast.

I got the rest of the story from the paper too. It was another short local news filler and it didn't say much, just that a fishboat had been found drifting near Stuart Island. The fisherman was missing, presumed drowned. The boat was the Lisa out of North Vancouver. I remembered what Pat had told me about the name on the stern of your boat being the last thing you see.

Only a sharp reporter would have put the two stories together and even if one had, it would still be tough to make a human interest piece that would pass a city editor out of the official facts; a bunch of parrots strangled and laid out in a row and a small commercial fishboat doing the Mary Celeste in an upcoast channel. The regulars in The Blue Parrot knew better and had more to say, accompanied by sagely wagged heads, but they kept the volume down. Marion was very quiet that night and, I suppose, so was I. Only when we'd finally steered the last stumbling guest at the impromptu wake out the doors and locked down, she looked a bit shaky, so I put my hand on her waist, just for comfort.

"Marion..." I started to say.

She spun on her spikes and flat-handed me across the face hard enough to fill the dark empty lounge with little flashing lights, like stinging fire-flies. That's what they call The End of Conversation. I stepped back behind the bar and applied a medicinal dose of eighty-proof Novocain for the soul, taken internally. A minute or two later, she came to the bar.

"I'm sorry," she said softly, "It's not your fault..."

We spend most of our lives waiting for someone to come along and tell us it's not our fault. By the time somebody does, we're past the point where we can believe it. I turned out the bar lights and opened the staff door.

The Blue Parrot

"Drink up, pal," I said, "It's closing time."

Felix lappped the last half-inch of his drink and darted between my legs and up the narrow stairs toward our room.

"Your poor face..." Marion said, as she stepped into the dingy deserted lobby. She reached to touch my cheek, but I turned away, pulling the door until I heard it click and lock. I walked up the stairs and this time I didn't look back.

Searchers found Pat's body a few days later. There were no obvious injuries. The inquest verdict was "death by misadventure". I thought that about covered it. I went to the funeral at Boal Chapel, up by the old North Van cemetery on Lillooet Road. Pat's son, Rick, was there, holding the arm of a very ordinary looking middle aged woman who I assumed was his mother. He was in black, appropriate as well as fashionable, but he had a good excuse for taking no notice of me for a change. First, I got suddenly furious when I saw him. I wanted to do something to hurt him, but after I saw what was in his face, I realized he didn't need any help from me.

At least the eulogy wasn't the usual platitudes delivered by some well-meaning divinity school graduate who never met the deceased and whose comments are as natural as the undertaker's makeup job. Instead, the young minister just read the old short service for the Burial At Sea and let it go at that. By the time he got to the part about how the sea shall give up its dead, I didn't even hate Lisa anymore. The best thing you can say about a funeral is that the guest of honour would have approved.

Lisa wasn't at the funeral. She's never come back into The Blue Parrot. I admit there have been a couple of times, when the vodka is hitting clean and clear and cold, I've felt a chill finger-walk up my spine and looked up, expecting to see her standing there, wearing that rueful half-apologetic smile. I know it's just the vodka and vanity, wanting to believe it all meant as much to her as it did to me.

I don't really expect she'll ever come back and it won't matter now if she does. Somebody finally made the owners of the old hotel the offer they've been waiting for. It's going to be torn down and replaced by a sleek retail and residential tower that looks in the drawings like an early science fiction illustration of a Space Ark. We've all been given two months notice.

The regulars and the residents are taking it hard, naturally. They say one of the hardest things in life is to out-live your own children. I don't know about that, but at the current rate, we all seem to out-live our own worlds, until the part of it we still recognize shrinks down to the size of a room in an old hotel and finally, down to nothing at all.

The Aunts are moaning and wringing their hands and their collective sherry intake has at least doubled. Mind you, I keep giving them drinks on the house. I figure they need it. Their relatives are putting them into "homes", a fate they speak of with the enthusiasm of heretics for the Inquistion, and they're entitled to something to steady their nerves.

I ran into Old Al outside the hotel on the day of Pat's funeral. He was wearing a black armband and I mentioned I thought it was a nice old-fashioned gesture to Pat's memory. I didn't recall seeing him at the service.

"Had another planting to see to," he announced, tapping the black crepe band, "My saw-bones finally slipped his cable."

He didn't seem overly concerned about his imminent eviction.

"I expect I'll be getting a berth any day now,' he said, with the understandable optimism of a man who has survived his physician.

Marion already has another job lined up at another deteriorating hotel a couple of blocks east of Lonsdale. She's staying one jump ahead of the wrecking-ball, at least. Helen's husband has bounced back like a bad cheque with a timely solution for her, pointing out that if she stops working and goes on welfare, she can get enough money to support them both as long as he doesn't actually move back in with her and the kids. With his undeclared income from various not very specific "deals", they'll be moving to separate lodgings on Easy Street in no time. I've got a little money socked away and with my severance and pogey, it'll be a while before I have to start applying for jobs slinging drinks in trendy night clubs where the sound system makes your ears bleed but it doesn't matter because the patrons are all too young and too beautiful to have anything to say.

Felix and I will have to find someplace to live. Fred, the Manager, gave me a hard time about keeping him in my room at first, litter box or no litter box, but when our notice came through, he shrugged it off and said, "What the fuck do I care? Keep a fucking giraffe, if you want."

It's too bad, really. Felix has become a regular fixture around the old place. He earns his drink, putting in a full shift reducing the rodent population in the rooms and corridors before he settles in behind the bar, and the old residents, especially The Aunts, are very taken with having him visit their rooms on his patrols. It's opened up a new arena of competition for them, each one seeking the mark of his favour by secretly bribing him with offerings of canned shrimp, tuna, tinned sockeye and bits of chicken boiled in cream. It takes their minds off the inevitable and no amount of luxury seafood seems to blunt his killer instinct. The building should be completely rodent-free about the time they pull it down.

I don't imagine we'll have any trouble finding a place. There are always basement suites for rent along the waterfront in North Van and I want Felix to be near the alleys, docks and railyards he knows. Maybe he'll stay and maybe he'll choose the company of his own wild kind. I'm not trying to get rid of him. He's good company, holds his drink better than most people and doesn't bore you rigid with his personal problems. I'd just like him to know that freedom is no further away than the back door.

In the meantime, we've got each other and the long quiet hours between two a.m. and dawn, and the cooler under the bed stocked with ice and vodka and Kahlua and cream. Sometimes I think about Pat and Lisa and about all the people who go through life looking for something they'll never find because they wouldn't know what to do with it if they held it in their hands. I think about all the debris they leave behind them, the ex-husbands and ex-wives, deserted houses, fostered children, forsaken friends and forgotten pets.

John Moore

I drink until I feel myself floating on a cold transparent river and the only thing wrong with going with the flow, as far as I can see, is that like water, you're always going downhill.

I don't know what Felix thinks of it all. He drinks and nods off in the crook of my arm, purring and growling like an old cat hunting phantom mice through the endless corridors of sleep. In the dark, while he dreams, I practise the sign language of the deaf and dumb and study the fading map of the gone world.